I0749380

ricepaper

CURRENTS

RICEPAPER MAGAZINE BOOKS VOLUME 1

KARLA COMANDA   LEILA LEE   WILLIAM THAM

ACWW   rp   DARK HELIX PRESS

Asian Canadian Writers Workshop publishes Ricepaper Magazine year round online. Visit Ricepapermagazine.ca for more details.

For permission requests, in correspondence, please send to "Attention: Editor-in-Chief," at the address below.

Ricepaper Magazine PO Box 74174 Centre Point Mall PO Vancouver, BC V5T 4E7

Alternatively: info@ricepapermagazine.ca www.ricepapermagazine.ca

Second Edition

Library and Archives Canada Cataloguing in Publication

Title: Currents / edited by Karla Comanda, Leila Lee, and William Tham ; cover art by Priscilla Yu ; book design by Keyan Zhang.

Other titles: Currents (Ricepaper Magazine)

Names: Comanda, Karla, 1985- editor. | Lee, Leila, 1986- editor. | Tham, William, 1991- editor.

Description: 2nd edition. | Series statement: Ricepaper Magazine books, 2562-4512 ; volume 1 | Poems and short stories. | Previously published: 2017.

Identifiers: Canadiana (print) 20190093560 | Canadiana (ebook) 20190093994 | ISBN 9781988416243

(softcover) | ISBN 9781988416267 (ebook)

Subjects: LCSH: Canadian literature—21st century. | LCSH: Asians—Canada—Literary collections. |

CSH: Canadian literature (English)—21st century. | CSH: Canadian literature (English)—Asian-Canadian authors.

Classification: LCC PS8235.A8 C87 2019 | DDC C810.8/0895071—dc23

Ricepaper Magazine Books

Immersion: An Asian Anthology of Love, Fantasy, and Speculative Fiction - Ricepaper Magazine Books Vol 2

The Seven Muses of Harry Salcedo by Vincent Ternida

Ricepaper Magazine (online)
ricepapermagazine.ca

FOR JIM WONG-CHU

In 1997, *Ricepaper Magazine* began life as the newsletter of the Asian Canadian Writers' Workshop.

Within a few years, it had grown to a quarterly magazine, showcasing works from many of the best Asian Canadian writers.

For 20 years we have shown that we can do anything.

We've examined the ideas of race and belonging, and studied what makes us both Asian and Canadian.

Today we continue our journey.

This is Ricepaper.

CONTENTS

Foreword xv
Introduction xix

1. Up North by Frances Du 1
2. Wake by Céline Chuang 3
3. Japanese Cheese by Jane Komori 11
4. marrow by Mary Chen 17
5. De Vivre Sa Vie by Aaron Tang 19
6. An Uncomplicated Whiteness by Benjamin Hertwig 27
7. Two Poems by Helen Tran 31
8. Three Microaggressions by JF Garrard 33
9. Carrying the Soul back Home by Zeng Xiaowen 35
10. Pritong Isda by Aileen Santos 41
11. The Dike by Carousel Calvo 43
12. From Whom the Maple Leaves Turn Red by Anna Wang Yuan 51
13. Become a Butterfly and Fly by Cheonhak Kwon 59
14. Crooked Teeth by Dung Kai-cheung 61
15. 9 Meditations on Poetry & Mandopop by Jasmine Gui 73
16. On Loss by Joanne Leow 79
17. Pre-Elementary, My Dear Monkey by Linda Nguyen 81
18. What I Learned from My Piano Lessons by Li Charmaine Anne 89
19. A Curve in Constellation by Stanford Cheung 95
20. Artefacts, Two Ways by Raine Ling 99
21. Dispatches from Nowhere by Kawai Shen 105
22. Confession of a Catholic's Daughter at the Temple of Au Co, Thirty-Five Years Post-Exodus by Do Nguyen Mai 109
23. A Collection of Rooms by Emi Kodama 111
24. the gardener by Lisa Zhang 119
25. Homecoming by Hannah Polinski 121
26. About Our Contributors 129
    "We can do anything" 137
27. About Our Team 139

FOREWORD

20 years, to quote Jim Wong-Chu, is an eternity in the magazine business.

Over the years, *Ricepaper* has taken many shapes and forms. We started as the official newsletter of the Asian Canadian Writers' Workshop, an organization which evolved from a student group at the University of British Columbia advocating for more inclusive representation in academia. We have served as a platform for various emerging and established writers, many of whom are now widely established and respected international literary figures. Through the articles that we have published, you can trace your way from Vancouver through the prairies and all the way to Toronto, Montréal, and the East Coast.

Transitioning into the digital age, we made the difficult decision to close our print edition last year and restructured *Ricepaper* into one of

Canada's leading Asian Canadian digital magazines with a new team of editors. As we continue to work towards building a strong online community for the Asian diaspora, we have made a conscious decision to broaden our definition of what it means to be Asian. Instead of looking inward and drawing from our pool of local writers, we have started looking for contributors and writers from across the globe. By doing so, we can listen to previously untold stories, allowing us to deepen our understanding of an increasingly intricate world.

2017 marks a special year for Canada. It seems fitting that we return to print in an anthology that will set the tone for the next stage of our evolution on the 150th anniversary of Confederation. However, this does not mean that we forget the various struggles that dominate Asian Canadian communities, not just in literature but also politically and historically. The pieces that you read here today are representations and reminders of our current state, which we hope will serve as a cornerstone for a new generation of writers.

Our selection of short stories, poetry, and nonfiction reflects our collective experience as members of the Asian diaspora and settlers of Canada. They are pulled from the articles we have published last year. We open up with sights and sounds — the expanses of the north, the coastal cities of the Lower Mainland, and the arid deserts of British Columbia's Interior. Mary Chen's "Marrow" takes us to the familiar streets of Vancouver in an exploration of the forgetfulness of generations and the fading past. Céline Chuang's "Wake" transports the reader away into a world of literal and figurative islands, touching briefly on the diaspora in various parts of the world. Do Nguyen Mai's haunting "Confessions of a Catholic's Daughter" takes us back through time into a fragmenting postcolonial world. The latter selections engage with common struggles and questions that transcend both time and place such as Kawai Shen's "Dispatches from Nowhere" and Joanne Leow's "On Loss." But ultimately, the idea that appears to capture the interest of many Asian writers is the search for belonging and a sense of "home." Henceforth we chose to close off with Hannah Polinski's "Homecoming."

We hope that you will enjoy this selection of pieces from us. Stories are not meant to be kept quiet, privately hidden away. Now they belong to you too. We hope that this is only the start of another 20 years of groundbreaking work.

Karla Comanda, Leila Lee, William Tham
Vancouver, BC, and Seoul, South Korea.
March 2017

INTRODUCTION

BY CHRISTOPHER LEE

"Where are you from?"

For many Asian Canadians, this seemingly innocent but famously vexed question captures an inescapable crisis of identity and belonging. As many of us have personally experienced, answers such as"Vancouver," "Toronto," "Moose Jaw," or "Montréal" are met with quizzical stares followed by the inevitable, "no, where are you really from?" Staged repeatedly in our daily lives, this awkward moment is stinging in its banality, for it is a moment when the feeling of belonging that we have relied on to live in this society is revealed to be an illusion. This scene suggests that we have always been, and perhaps will always be, seen as "foreign" rather than an integral part of what we had thought was our place in the world. From writers, scholars, artists, and activists, we have learned that this moment follows a script that has been shaped through more than a century of exclusion policies, denial of civil rights, rejection of asylum seekers, and economic as well as cultural discrimination. But seen against the background of Canada's colonial history, our desire to be recognized as Canadian can obscure more difficult questions about the role of Asian migrants in the dispossession of Indigenous peoples, or the fraught meaning of citizenship in a globalizing world. So while the desire for national belonging and politics of racial exclusion have understandably been at the heart of Asian Canadian culture, these issues can obscure the complex histories that have shaped our presence on this land. The ongoing challenge, ably embraced by so many writers, cultural producers, and activists, is still to imagine an Asian Canadian cultural practice that can be expansive enough to address the ongoing legacies of racism without losing sight of resonances and relationalities that tie us to other communities.

When I was growing up, these issues were rarely talked about either at home or at school. Even though I attended a high school with students from around the world, my immigrant family experience always seemed somehow peripheral to the dominant culture around me. In university, I became an English major, but being steeped in the great classics of British literature did not exactly yield a better understanding of the migrations that had brought my family, and so many families that I knew, to Canada. It was around this time that I discovered the groundbreaking works of writers such as SKY Lee, Wayson Choy, Larissa Lai, Terry Watada, Phinder Dulai, Roy Miki, Joy Kogawa, Fred Wah, and many others. The summer after my second year, I got a job at a pulp mill in a small isolated town north of Vancouver, where slow pace gave me hours of free time to read. Perched in a corner of the machinery shop where I worked, I experienced the excitement of finding writers who looked like me and who told stories that resonated with my own. On weekends, I went back to Vancouver and started to attend readings and other community events. At one of these events, I met Jim Wong-Chu, who encouraged me to write for *Ricepaper*, which was at the time the newsletter of the Asian Canadian Writer's Workshop. Despite its then-limited readership, for a newbie like me, *Ricepaper* was a window into a literary world that I had only just encountered but now couldn't imagine not existing. Before long, I had written my first review (of a book by David Suzuki) and later that summer, I got to interview Jan Wong, Wayson Choy, and Adrienne Clarkson for *Ricepaper*, even though only the last interview ended up being published.

These experiences would prove to be pivotal as I went on to graduate school and became an academic. For the past decade, I have taught Asian Canadian and Asian diaspora literatures at UBC where my students and I are still grappling with questions about culture, identity, and belonging, sometimes by reading the same novels that had captivated me when I was their age. Living in a city with historically deep ties to the Asia Pacific, the question "Where are you from" has become (actually ... it has always been) much more complicated, as dominant narratives of immigration as a one-way trajectory and settlement and assimilation fall apart against the realities of multiple migrations on a global scale. Asian Canadians are, in deep and profound ways, from elsewhere. As settlers on various Indigenous territories, we are implicated in histories of dispossession and violence, both within and beyond the borders of the nation. At the same time, racialized exclusion has not disappeared and continues to be compounded by issues of gender, sexuality, and class. Asian Canadian culture, while flourishing, often remains peripheral to the national conversation, and the representation of Asian Canadian artists, writers, and cultural producers continues to be uneven. Against these complexities, I wonder whether there might be a day when it will be safe to ask an Asian Canadian where he or she is from, when the question will no longer be saturated with exclusionary assumptions but instead function as an invitation to listen to different stories of migration and imagine relationships within and beyond communities and nations.

Reading *Currents* gives me a glimpse of what that conversation might look like. This collection is a powerful reminder that Asian Canadians come from a lot of places, some of which are not located in either Canada or lands of origin in Asia. Together, these points of passage constitute the meandering itineraries that have brought us to this place, some temporarily and others less so. Many of the pieces are searing indictments of discrimination, a reminder that our lives continue to be shaped by the historical legacies of racism. Embedded in these pages are scenes of desire and alienation, connection and empathy. Some pieces depict poverty, conflict, desperation, and loss while others are full of humour, indignation, or reflection. Again and again, *Currents* reminds me of the power of language, particularly literary language, in making us aware of the fullness of our lives as historical and embodied subjects. As I was reading, I was constantly struck by its aesthetic range — that breathtaking poetic line or turn of phrase, the unexpected plot twist, the profound insight that makes you put down the book and just sit with the words resounding in your mind.

For more than twenty years, *Ricepaper* has offered a safe, if not always comfortable, place to explore these issues and *Currents* is a fantastic tribute to the many voices that have crossed its pages. By reminding us of the power of the written word to help us see Asian Canadian lifeworlds in new and surprising ways, it invites us to attend to stories of migration that traverse boundaries of ethnicity, language, and nationality. It prompts us to imagine what it would be like to live lives that are more rich, more just, more free. While *Currents* can only capture a slice of what has been published in *Ricepaper*, everything that this collection suggests tells me that there is so much more to come. And for that we should all be very grateful.

Christopher Lee is the Director of the Asian Canadian and Asian Migration Studies Program (ACAM) at the University of British Columbia.

1

UP NORTH BY FRANCES DU

We take the scenic route.
Heading up North the land dotted with wildlife, farms the size of stadiums, one that sells only eggs,
the other, wild blueberries. Rocks ahead break out from their shells,
forming fissures, jagged lines you want to smooth
with your hands, the color of thyme and cinnamon.
Breathing in the air is like gaining new lungs untouched by the city
lit with gas and oil. It's so nice and we are only five miles away, two pit stops,
family van driving past Muskoka to the tip where there are mountains
and waterfalls if you're thirsty. There's Twiggs,
the only coffee shop in town, a store for party favors, another for
Momma Poon's Thai Food. Everyone sleeps at 8.
If you want to watch the sunset go to King's Landing, not the other
one by the Super 8; that's where all the derelicts go.
There are the kids and the newlywed, but most are retired
and head South during the winter. The cold can be brutal here
but that seems like an imaginary thought in this summer heat which
noses its way into every crevice and contour of the body, denimed out.

There are the boats, the rivers rats. There are the regulars having chili
and salad at Swiss Chalet, the lone movie theater.
10 minutes out of town, a strawberry field ripe for picking.
We trample inside. A young redhead making jam is bewildered
by my face, my otherness. The waitress recommends at dinner:
how about the Oriental chicken?
She means nothing by it but everywhere we go, eyes follow,
landing on our squid ink hair, pinching our arms.
We watch a bachelorette party unfold at a table behind us.
These girls have known each other forever, bedazzled
and bemoaning time passing, trading grade school gems, stories about
the unfuckable. When the bugs come out, we rally inside. On the drive
back we try to decide on
what to make with all those berries. Maybe jam or a milkshake.
My sister whispers into my ear, the moonlight glinting off her necklace.
Maybe even a pie.

2

WAKE BY CÉLINE CHUANG

I

Rain is blurring windshields and spitting from street side sewers the day Benoît arrives at the airport. His nut-coloured face floats abreast of the huddle of arrivals and when he sees me he smiles with almond eyes squashing upwards, showing no teeth.

"You've done something stupid with your hair again," I tell him. I push my fingers through the garish blue stripe over the crown of his head, map out the bumps of his skull. His hair is soft and crinkly like old coffee filters.

"Yeah, I cut it." He stoops to hug me, pressing his nose into my shoulder. He looks older, spine curved by the heaviness of long flights, bad posture, and the appropriation of grief as it has been handed along the family tree in portions. There are a lot of us, plenty to go around. Back in Vacoas, Poh Poh used to make rice balls with black bean sauce in the only pot she had and the thick charcoal-coloured liquid would seep into the broth as she stirred it. Rough wooden spoon in her sinewy little arm. There was always enough for dessert. *Mangez, mangez!* she would say, forcefully waving us over with the spoon. Dessert is like grief in this way, the way our family has doled it into bowls and fought over the rest with false martyrdom.

"Who did it for you?" I pull back a little to stare at him again, his fisherman pants and dip-dyed t-shirt. "God, you look like a hip-hop dancer." I wonder, too quickly, whether he picked out his outfit before or after he heard the news about Kung Kung. Then guilt seeps in, flooding the bottom of my stomach.

"A girl in LA," he smiles. Still no teeth. "It's good to see you, Addi."

"You too, Benny." I mash my face into the soft t-shirt fabric and fight the quiver. I always hated crying in airports. Benoît smells faintly like dry sun and sweat, California hitchhiking on his skin. We stand there as others mill around us going to the baggage carousel. I can feel my spine beginning to curve.

2

"Addi," I can hear Benny yelling, "did you put my wool socks through the wash?"

I clunk through the kitchen with the laundry basket, stubbing my toe and swearing."Yeah!" I yell back between muffled expletives. The apartment has shrunk with Benny here. There are shoes everywhere, in various cultivated neutrals and the occasional neon eyesore (high- tops). How these fit into his suitcase is a miracle of physics, or maybe a touch of Caribbean voodoo.

Creole syllables jumble under my bedroom door. He must be skyping his mum. Yi Yi Ah Lai's Creole is less abrasive than the other aunties, you can hear echoes of her school-taught French in it. At family reunions the jabbering is all a pile of animated accents, the edges of French bitten off, chewed, and regurgitated over steaming curries and fried fish. Poh Poh looking on, bemused, chewing toothlessly.

Benny's arguing with her about something. My Creole's rusty, but when I hear my name amidst her rapid-fire chatter I retreat back to the kitchen and drop off the basket of clean clothes outside his door.

Back in the kitchen, the pile of dirty dishes teeters. It vaguely resembles an inukshuk.

I look around at the open pancake mix box and half-empty bottle of whiskey on the formica. My makeshift bed on the couch with its mess of blankets and half-open laptop glow. Outside, the rain falls thickly, catching on lashes of pine. In the silence, I am suddenly, awfully dwarfed by the magnitude of grief, of its stark wilderness. Afraid to breathe, almost, to move and dislocate myself completely from the pulse of voices down the hallway. What kind of vacuum would it be to lose track of myself and become part of the still life?

I wait, paralyzed, for Benny to emerge and offer to make me another homemade cocktail, or help me do the dishes. We could sink up to our elbows in bubbles and look out at the night like older, gentler winters when his family and mine were together for Christmas.

I wait until it's almost dark. My right foot has fallen asleep. Benny's room is quiet and the house is slanted with shadows. I turn off the stove light and leave the dishes.

Poh Poh and Kung Kung left their Hakka village in Southeastern China at the height of the Communist regime. They had a bag between them. Their slippers wore down to the straw. Poh Poh and Kung Kung walked miles in the dark, through mountains and rivers and the ash of their ancestors. Saving matches for the darkest hours and bickering about their choice.

"We will have many children," Kung Kung said to Poh Poh, walking ahead. He didn't hold her hand.

"Yes," Poh Poh grunted, "and they will be safer where we're going. We can do what we want there."

"We don't speak the language," Kung Kung said. He carried his Johnnie Walker black label and a carton of cigarettes in his pocket. Poh Poh carried the bag, strapped across her body like a child.

"Who cares," Poh Poh said. She pulled up the bag strap and walked on. "Our children will." They slipped through the dark sheaves of long grass and thick summer air, tethered to each other by their parents' alliance and instinct for survival. They would take a boat, she told herself, they would be rattled by ocean and stifled by heat but they would be free.

. . .

It's two in the afternoon when I get back from my shift at the diner and Benny's room is still silent. I look at the stratum that has accumulated from one week and feel the hot, peppery surge of anger boil up despite my mental efforts to quash it.

When I bang into his room without knocking he's cross-legged, meditating.

"Oh, come on." I kick aside a pile of crumpled clothes. "Will you help me clean up the kitchen or what. Since when did you do yoga?"

"Since two weeks after I moved to LA," he snipes. "You wrecked my vibe, I was trying to nurture the positive. Can you please knock next time? If you're so upset just tell me goddammit. I could hear you banging around the kitchen all yesterday."

"I was banging around because of the mess."

"Oh, I'm so sorry you're so worried about organization right now."

"You would think for someone so trendy and LA you would care more about feng shui. You're like a hobo with a hoarding addiction, God."

Benny stares at me. "The fuck got into you? I'm here, I'm staying out of your hair."

"That's what you always do. That's what you did, you know, you never were at Vacoas, you were off in Portland or Toronto or LA and everyone thought that was ok."

"If I came to all those family things I'd go crazy for God's sake. You agreed with me, remember we talked it about it over the phone. We sit around and eat and Kung Kung would never even talk. He would watch his TV and smoke and drink and occasionally yell something at us in Chinese."

"I know, I visited him!"

"So did I. So did I, Addi, so what the hell is your issue? Why are you crying?"

"Why are you here then?"

"What are you talking about?"

"Why — " I stop, and the word hangs there. "Why are you here. If you aren't going to." The rest of the sentence gets lost somewhere and dangles horribly in the empty air. I swipe at leaking eyes, refuse to let myself look at the ground.

Benny looks at me carefully. "I'm here," he says, as clearly as he can. In English, and then Creole. He stands up, still wary, but with a softness around his eyes. "Come on, let's make rougaille for lunch."

3

Poh Poh and Kung Kung moved into Vacoas, a small town by both Chinese and Mauritian standards. They bought a house, put up fences, bought guard dogs and chickens and clotheslines. Poh Poh had eight children, including Benny's mum and my mum. Because they were the poorest in the middle of having all their kids, mum is the smallest. If you lined up all eight aunties, their heights would form a V. Poh Poh sent all of them to school, where they were taught in French. Outside school, neighbours, storekeepers, and friends spoke Creole. None of the aunties, the Yi Yis, can speak Chinese of any kind. Poh Poh and Kung Kung learned some Creole, grudgingly, painstakingly. Enough to say *mangez*, enough to say hurry up, sit down, go to sleep.

"Eight daughters," Kung Kung said to Poh Poh in Hakka as she cooked dinner.

"Yes, and they are strong." Poh Poh didn't look at Kung Kung. When he was sitting in his TV chair with his striped pyjamas on he was extra stubborn.

"Eight daughters," he repeated."Was it too much to ask for one son." He changed the channel. "I should have gone to the temple more. I didn't pray enough."

"The ancestors can't change what was in here," Poh Poh said, patting her stomach. She was lean again, having shed pregnancy like the new outfits she could not afford. "Get your feet off the table."

The house on the island creaked and bent at the seams with eight girls, all craning their necks for a glimpse of the world. Eventually it became too much. The house stayed, but the girls went. Mum and Benny's mum and our oldest aunt, Yi Yi Ah Fin, held out the longest. Yi Yi Ah Fin still lives with Poh Poh and brings her milk, settles her into bed, and watches soap operas with her between breakfast and lunch. She straightens the photos of all the cousins on the wall. We're right below a cardboard icon of the Madonna and Child. Poh Poh goes to the Temple but likes to keep the icon on the wall just in case.

Benny's dad was a good Mauritian boy, Creole and casually Catholic, not well versed in pop culture or poetry. But he could work a fishing boat and a catamaran over the reefs with one hand. Yi Yi Ah Lai stayed with him as long as she could, but university — and the Beatles — were calling. Dad was a British lawyer who'd attended a wedding in Port Louis where mum was catering. When mum woke up she looked at Dad and said, damn, found myself my own grand blanc. Later, in one of those improbable rom-com-cum-real-life moments, she found him in a coffee place in London. Benny's mum and her had jumped ship from Mauritius when we were around seven or eight.

I still remember waking up to heavy fog and honking horns and wondering if Vacoas was something I made up. All throughout middle school I would dream of palm fronds combing blue skies, sugar-cane breezes and Poh Poh's sweet black bean soup, the sharpness of overripe mangoes in the marketplace. Searing sunsets that lingered on the rim of the ocean as if the world were ending every night. Sometimes I still have them, sudden and bruising, wake up sore like I've been underwater and struggling to surface.

Benny and I visited Poh Poh and Kung Kung after the move, but not together. I hopped on a plane to Vancouver on the way to a boy I thought I was in love with in Prince George. Instead, I never left the city. Benny eventually ended up in LA, writing music reviews. Apart from occasionally cruising his blog, I never saw him. We became Benoît and Adelaide again. All of the Yi Yis gave their kids French names.

4

I wake up in the night shaking the couch with sobs, my body wrenching itself in half. The moon is low on the horizon and the tears on my pillow look dusty red. I am convulsing so hard I can't breathe, can't think, can't name where or who I am. Only slowly and inexorably being crushed to the sheets by the darkness just outside the window, pressurized into white noise, lost, languageless. The air is hot, suffused with a sweetness that sticks to my tongue. In this moment I suddenly know, wildly and with the clarity of a gunshot, that I was wrong in the airport. Familial grief is not portioned and passed down out of duty. It sinks through branches in the family tree like blood and varicose veins and rears, ugly and tidal, where the limbs end. At the generation just learning to walk out of its grandparents' shoes. I taste salt, bite my tongue. My feet twist uselessly in blankets, my mind blank, my eyes filling and filling with tears that aren't mine.

Benny's here, without being called for, rolls into the onion layers of blankets like he belongs. He finds me under the reddish light and curls his body around me. Just like cousin sleepovers in Vacoas when one of us had nightmares after a scary movie. I smooth into seaglass stillness. The distance between continents yawns open again, the static ceases. The image of Poh Poh rocking back and forth in her chair, hands clasped tight, fades.

It's Benny's turn now. I used to be the stronger one. When we were little he would paw at my face during scary movies and ask "Is it real Addi? Is it real?" and I'd say, "No, it doesn't happen in real life" and turn him in my arms, tuck him into me until he fell asleep.

Now, he doesn't say anything, but shakes out his portion of the sorrow. I flip us and hold him and fall asleep against his back. He smells clean, like laundry and open skies, the barest hint of nutmeg. For the first time, he smells familiar.

5

Benny and I sit on the coach with our feet up. He's wearing his wool socks.

"I can't believe you bought me an herb garden," I say. I'm looking in disbelief and slight admiration at the shallow silver basin on the counter with its burst of leaves overflowing from dark soil." All I said was that I needed basil. You could have bought the dry stuff."

"That stuff is shit," Benny says. He's polishing off the coconut curry with shameless slurps that make Yi Yi Ah Lai would proud. "Plus now you have some of the real stuff for the future."

The fridge starts whirring. The kitchen, lit by light, looks less sterile with the coffeepot half-full and the piles of inukshuk dishes. I don't need to be told I've acclimatized to the clutter. It will all be put away later. And the invasion of bare counter and empty space is a relief, proof of company. I've never been so glad to have my landscape marred.

"When are you leaving?" The words feel sticky and clumsy as I work them through my gums into the air. I look sideways at Benny. He puts his bowl down and pulls me sideways into him. I rest my cheek on his shoulder and try to swallow. Outside the apartment, the skytrain hums past and everything moves an inch to the left. The curtains flutter with yellow glow, and the dishes shift and sigh.

"What was the last thing he said to you?" I ask, almost under the noise.

Benny pauses, licks mango chutney off his fingers. "Pass the peanuts," he says.

I laugh, startling him. He jumps, then grins. The night glimmers with white teeth and the promise of a fellow passenger into the labyrinths ahead. No longer solitary, chasing what the water leaves behind. Fifty-two years ago, a boat bumps the shore. Poh Poh and Kung Kung step onto smooth sand and red rock, holding hands.

3

JAPANESE CHEESE BY JANE KOMORI

Japanese Cheese was named in the hills above Westsyde where Dad and his friends dirt bike through Ponderosa pines and thickets of sagebrush. Low, rounded mountains encircle the valley in which the city of Kamloops nestles, straddling the confluence of the North and South Thompson Rivers. To the west, perhaps visible from where the dirt bikers stopped to rest, my grandparents' property spans an acre of rambling garden, rock sculptures twice the height of the house, and a precarious unfinished gazebo.

The dirt bikers roll to a stop so that Dad can pull sweating packages of cheddar from his Camelback and offer them to the group. The valley radiates heat in summer, catching it in its bowl and throwing it back into the cloudless sky. The smell of the aged cheese is amplified by dry heat and it begins to cling to the edges of the soft plastic packaging, losing its uniform, sterile shape. While peeling off the wrappers and taking bites between sips from the Camelback's teat, one of the men in Dad's dirt biking company cries, "Hey, Donny! What the fuck is this? Some kind of Japanese cheese?"

The Japanese Cheese, as it was known from then on, appears at every outdoor activity, in packed lunches, and during long car trips. This February, at the end of a rolling hike across Ruckle Provincial Park on Salt

Spring Island, we settle on a stretch of rock, worn smooth and undulating by the Salish Sea. "I brought the Japanese Cheese!" Dad declares triumphantly as we recline at the edge of the ocean. He never forgets, announcing the cheese with a self-assuredness that perplexes me. The way the short 'a' and long 'e' of Japanese are drawn out, the soft consonants whistling through relaxed lips and teeth. "Japan" sounds smooth, rolling off a tongue coated in the saliva that Balderson Royal Canadian Cheddar elicits in the mouth. The nationality, the suffix "ese," presents like a soft exhale at the end of the first bite. We tilt ourselves toward the distant winter sun, already descending. Ever prepared, Dad swings his Camelback from his Gore-Tex clad shoulder, offering me the mouthpiece. We ignore the motherly gesture; the Camelback is purely practical; its compact and ergonomic form carries three liters of water and snacks. Snacks we have in abundance — salted cashews, EatMore bars, peanut butter cookies, and doughy bagels from Safeway. Dad is having a weekend away and so we need French pastries, a "family-sized" bag of plain Lay's chips, five bottles of wine, steak and béarnaise sauce, mochi with sugar and soy sauce, and the Japanese Cheese.

This summer, "Donny," as Dad is known to his biking crew, will host the dirt bikers for his end of summer pool party. They arrive en masse each August, children and cousins in tow. Ken describes his failed marriage at length, washing each story down with a Corona. Brendan, Ken's son who used to cut the lawn, eats too much cheese before hitting the bong and throwing up over the side of the hot tub. Toddlers hang from mothers' arms in the shallow end while the men do backflips off the small diving board to AC/DC. One year, the party fell shortly after my last surgery to fix my cleft lip and palate and I barricaded myself in my room, puffy and embarrassed. Another year, I walked into the kitchen just as a dirt biking friend of a friend tried to sling his arm around my sister's waist. Mom, my sister, and I dread the party, agonizing for months over whether or not to invite friends as a buffer, a reprieve, or as more fuel for the fire.

Japanese Cheese in the heat smells and feels like a childhood summer camp that took us all on a walk through Kenna Cartwright Park the day that I wore sandals. I pulled cactus spines from my toes the whole drive home. The sandals were the kind Mom rarely allowed: new, purple, strappy, and covered in sparkles. Beautiful, before they were covered in red desert dust and tiny constellations of blood where the prickles had lodged themselves in my feet. Recently, she has taken to complimenting me on my more practical taste in footwear. "I knew you would come around," she says. I tend to think, in August, of all of the sopping, miserably sun-baked sandwiches that accompanied me to those summer camps that would be eaten quickly and alone because of the way they dripped down my elbows and onto my shorts, made hopelessly soggy by thick slices of ox heart tomatoes from Grandpa's garden. His tomatoes always split with their own ripeness, turning cat-faced and black from the heat of the greenhouse. Grandma crouches, sweating, at five AM each summer day, picking fat white larvae from the open seams of each fruit.

Grandma once gave me a kilogram of Japanese Cheese wrapped in saran wrap to take back to Vancouver on the Greyhound. I forgot the cheese on her counter, and she called the next day to tell me that she had only just found it, mutilated by the Kamloops sun spilling through her kitchen window. Lately, Grandma has grown so fond of Babybel cheese that it threatens Japanese Cheese as the family favourite. She loves the neat puck shape wrapped in bright red wax. At her house over Christmas, I found half-peeled crescents of cheese on the bathroom counter beside the sink, in the drawer with her Sudoku books and pens, and on the altar of the Komori shrine.

Mom tells me about how Dad got drunk on Canada Day, at a small gathering on the banks of a creek in Turtle Valley, where family friends have spent every summer of their lives. "The creek is healing," a friend sighed as she eased herself into one of its wells, cold water rushing around up to her neck. Later, Dad prodded at steaks and sausages, while Mom tossed salads and opened jars of pickles and hummus. Dinner wore on around the campfire where Dad's rosy drunkenness went largely unnoticed until the Japanese Cheese was passed around. Dad told of its origins and reminded all of his white friends from Westsyde Secondary School; "When you see me, you see a Japanese person." His hosts stiffened in their nylon camp chairs. Everyone protested, and for once Dad was unrelenting.

"You know how you feel," he declared in a voice that hovered over the creek and campfire.

On Salt Spring Island, the route back to the truck is long and winding, leading us through dark cedar stands. The forest is so damp that our boots get stuck in deep black mud and our faces are covered in layers of dew. I called Dad in tears two years ago when I pulled a pile of clothes out of my closet only to discover they were covered in a wet grey dust, sifted all over like icing sugar. I wanted to know what was going on, why I was paying six hundred dollars for a wet room in a basement, why my clothes were being eaten away. "It's fucking moldy down there!" Dad proclaimed. In Kamloops, my and Dad's hands crack and bleed from the harsh desert. I could leave a pile of wet towels on the floor and expect to find them dry the next day. Open bags of potato chips sit on the counter for days and retain their crisp edges. I never woke up with a phlegmy cough, spitting yellow slime into a wastebasket next to my bed because of the rain that encroaches on every building in the city.

In January, Mom, Dad, my sister Rachel, and I flew to Winnipeg for a wedding. My cousin was marrying a Mennonite music therapist from Northern Manitoba. It was bitterly cold; we skated on the Red River, and fell so hard on our knees that the pain shot up our spines. Our middle cousin killed himself in the room adjacent to the guest room Rachel and I stayed in in our aunt and uncle's basement. The ceremony was held in a large church downtown during its Sunday evening service, so that our small family subset was forced to huddle in a back pew, where Dad nudged me and whispered, "Everyone in here is white." Dave and Judith handed out communion after saying their vows, and rows upon rows of family and friends crowded to the front of the church. Dad gestured towards a hallway at the back of the church where we hid for the remainder of the service.

Afterwards, Dad passed around a mickey of Fire Ball, disrupting the sobriety of the quiet reception in the church basement. Around plates of perogies, kuchen, and matrimonial cake, our cheeks blossomed with colour at the first sip. The perogies were filled with sauerkraut and cottage cheese. Grandma fills hers with mashed potatoes, Japanese cheese, and green onions. A few more sips, and we became blotchy with redness, our mottled skin giving us away as interlopers. The perogies congealed on my plate into greyish lumps that lodged homesickness in the back of my throat with each vinegary bite. As the night wears on we are made more and more self-conscious not only by our unruliness but also from wearing the rosacea handed down by ancestors who couldn't hold their liquor. Pink creeps down my neck and into my earlobes. Pink like the sun on a smoggy day in Osaka, around the time school would let out and I would take the long train ride home. At dinner during our last night on the island, Mom steps away from the table for a minute. Dad glances at me between bites of lobster ravioli to remind me that, "Everyone on the Islands is white, eh?" I nod, worn out from our weekend away. "I feel much more at home on the mainland." I want to talk about this, but Mom is already on her way back from the bathroom.

Two ferry rides and a four-hour drive later, we arrive in Kamloops. A sense of relief fills the truck as we move from coastal rainforest to the wetter interior mountains of Hope, across the icy Coquihalla Summit, and finally into the hills and plains of Kamloops. Patches of snow illuminate the bluish nighttime. Dad hopes that an early spring will have him dirt biking again by the end of the week. Grandma and Grandpa join us for dinner in our small, warm dining room with a view over the valley, from which their house is barely visible near the edge of the North Thompson River. We describe our trip: the French pastries, the long hike through Ruckle Provincial Park, and the fish and chips.

"That was half Japanese before the war!" Grandpa shouts. Nearly deaf, he mostly drifts in and out of conversations, interjecting with whatever comes to mind. Tonight, he has followed the trajectory of our stories closely, waiting to reveal his knowledge of the island. "They farmed and fished there. I been there," he declared, before returning to his steak.

The cabin we stayed in had a coffee table book about Salt Spring Island. The pages were filled with smiling organic farmers and craftsmen who grow perfect round tomatoes and build coffins and chandeliers out of driftwood.

That first night back at home in Kamloops, I realize that I have forgotten to unload the cooler once everyone else has already gone to bed. One of the ice packs has exploded a thick layer of slime, coating the bottom two inches of the bin. I pull out our weekend leftovers one by one, rinsing them off. A half-finished jar of Grandma's dill pickles. Mom's organic, unsalted peanut butter from Trader Joe's. I swish my fingers through the goo until I pull up several small, uniform, rectangular packets. The Japanese Cheese, sealed tight, is still cool to the touch. I sit down and stare at them, tinted an unearthly blue by the contents of the ice pack. There are little translucent beads in the blueness that glimmer like tiny marbles. On Salt Spring Island, the stars cast their light onto the beach.

4

MARROW BY MARY CHEN

when i left 婆婆's place
the sky was drooling like an infant cutting her first tooth a pink mess of sunset and saliva and tender throbbing warmth. the train cried as it hurtled the 27 minutes from seawall to sleepy suburb and i wanted so much to kiss its windows and say 我知道 but we were packed shoulder to armpit in that compartment and i was afraid of the things the white sea could spit at my feet.

i didn't know how to say
mri in chinese or how to explain the old age security form. why their subsidized bus pass would take another month to come into effect. once i took a popo to her cataract surgery and on the way home we passed the site where tamura house once stood where nothing lived now but splintered wood bones gone soft and slick with eastside mud. the popo took those bones dragged them home told me they would stop the roaches from crawling inside. what must we do so our seniors will no longer be pushed out of food lineups yelled at called dirty chinese on main and hastings? their old joints witnessed japanese imperialism groaned through childbirth now one popo tells me 我想死也死不了

while another smiles and says 我真是充滿了愛. both times i couldn't say anything back.

you deserve so much
more than impatient doctors mice under your beds children who have all grown up grown old forgotten the sound of 媽 coming from their own mouths. more than english drawing a line between those who deserve and those who take. more than silence.

5

DE VIVRE SA VIE BY AARON TANG

A cold winter gust brought him a familiar smell of perfume. He dropped his cigarette and softly pressed a finger against his nose. The smoke from his fingertips mingled with the fading scent of the woman. He turned, but the woman was lost in the crowd. He stood still in the busy winter street and lit another cigarette. The ashes fell, scattering over his shadow as he walked through the knotted streets of Tokyo, memories of memories whispered towards the past.

He was in Tokyo because of Izumi Nakamura.

Izumi wore a perfume with the soft smell of jasmine, and had a slight hint of smoke lingering about her. It was winter when he first met Izumi, but she had been wearing a simple, long, flowery red dress that revealed her shoulders. Her movements had been elegant, with nothing unnecessary. Her legs were the type that you wouldn't pay much attention to. They weren't especially long, but rather just right — the kind of legs that look perfect in heels. Her slightest movements, the tone of her voice, and the way she looked when she was listening, all came together to form a sense of inherent beauty. She had the kind of beauty that's in everyone's blood, but that is slowly fading more and more with each generation.

After the day they first met, they had started seeing each other every day. One day when they were straightening up his apartment, he found a black wooden box. He tended to throw out anything that he hadn't used in a while, but he had no memory of having this black box in his cupboard. Izumi opened it, and found that inside there were photographs of caves filled with light. After some research, they found out that these were photographs of mountain caves in New Zealand, called the Waitomo Glowworm Caves, where thousands of tiny larvae hung from the cave's ceiling, creating a luminescent effect. Those natural living lights had been glowing for centuries. She had always wanted to go to New Zealand. Since she was little, she had been fascinated with a huge extinct bird called the Moa, which had last been seen there. He found it strange that she could have such a passionate wish to visit somewhere simply because of something so long gone.

They worked hard throughout the summer, hoping to save enough money to go see the caves together. In the end, they made the money, but the trip was still impossible. They were both students from overseas. He was about to graduate, and was planning to return to Hong Kong to start his career. At their young age, establishing a place in society had seemed more important than any love they might encounter along the way. But, they thought, things are not supposed to end just like that. So they promised each other that they would meet ten years later at the caves.

Over that summer, they used the money that they had earned to visit each other. Then she returned to Tokyo and devoted herself to her career. He did the same in Hong Kong. They met new people and sought new opportunities with something like desperation. Things were never as they had once been. Life wore them out, and the passion they had both felt slowly faded away, as if it had been locked up in the cave by their promise... just like the cave lights. After so long he still hadn't been to New Zealand. He almost went once, a year and a half ago when he and his wife were on their honeymoon. They stayed at a friend's place in Sydney for a month, and his wife had suggested that they take a short trip to New Zealand together. She knew that he was interested in the place. He just told her that he'd rather spend more time in Australia.

Godard's *Vivre Sa Vie* was showing on the art-house film channel he subscribed to, precisely one week before the day the two were to meet. Izumi and he used to watch avant-garde films together all the time, and they would have long discussions about them afterwards. He hasn't watched many since. Now, ten years later, he was watching this one with his third scotch. Drinking as the film played, he closed his eyes. With the bit of French he learned in college, and having watched the film a couple of times, he still knew what was happening on the screen. It was the part where Anna Karina is being told what a little girl in a professor's class wrote to describe her favorite animal. "A bird is an animal with an outside and an inside. Take away the outside, the inside is left. Take away the inside, and you see the soul." He uttered the lines to himself a couple times. He was never fond of his own voice, and had found it to be rather dull. But for some reason, he liked how his voice sounded when he spoke those lines. As his voice echoed in the empty living room, he started to sense a vague presence of Izumi, and echoes of echoes surrounded him.

Drunk on the couch, he started thinking about Izumi. When they went out they would always find small restaurants. To them, the music that restaurants played was more important than whether the seats were comfortable, the smell of the coffee more important than the taste of the wine, and the small entrées fascinated them more than the main course. When you're young, you feel like you'll meet lots of people with whom you will truly connect, but as you get older, you realize that this only happens a few times.

That being said, his married life wasn't bad. His wife had a good job, and they owned a decent-sized apartment in the heart of Hong Kong with a great view of the vast harbor.

They met in their mid-twenties and got married at thirty. He had never been unfaithful to her before — but not for lack of opportunity, or because the women he met hadn't been attractive. He and his wife got along well, and they simply hadn't felt the need or desire to have affairs. He looked around the living room; everything in the apartment looked fine. The living room was nice and clean, but its white designer couch and its stylish, open-concept kitchen suddenly gave him a chill. He walked onto the balcony with his glass of scotch and stared across the water as the lights of the International Finance Centre slowly turned off, one after another.

Do places have souls?

Suddenly, the phone started ringing. He didn't want it to wake his wife, so he ran to pick it up. A man's voice greeted him by his last name. The man asked him to meet at a nearby bar. He wasn't at all surprised. He just thought it was his boss's new assistant. His boss changed assistants all the time, so he assumed that his boss wanted to try something new by hiring a man this time around. With a simple "Ok!" he put on his jacket and headed out without thinking about why he was getting such a call at that hour. He locked the door, walked to the lift, and pressed the button. The elevator's walls were made of glass, and as he dropped from the 47th floor he saw the lights from all the other nearby buildings flashing by. He was always freest when he was on that lift, truly himself without realizing it. Instead, when he was in there, he obliterated the present, as he was always trying to go somewhere else or to return to his apartment. He could always see his own reflection in its glass, so different from how he imagined himself. Walking outside that night, he saw his shadow and thought that it resembled the vision of himself that he kept in his mind's eye much more closely than it resembled the reality. Nothing existed beyond the surface of a shadow. At that moment, his reflection was shared with the thousand shining lights of the city... He had stepped out of the lift, and kept walking while his shadow led the way.

When he got to the bar, he saw a handsome young man in a perfectly pressed white shirt, blue chinos, and a shiny watch, sitting on the patio with an espresso. He was almost certain that this was the man who had called. The man seemed to have been waiting there for quite some time. He walked over to him; the man stood up to greet him and asked him to sit down.

"I see you're living well here, Isaiah. Nice apartment, nice area."

"It's all right, I guess," he answered. He was starting to realize that this man might not be his boss's assistant. A slight look of confusion appeared on his face.

There was a moment of silence.

The young man sipped his espresso. Then he looked at Isaiah and finally said, "Pardon me for not introducing myself. I just assumed that you would recognize me."

Isaiah looked at the young man's eyes. They were large and brown, with a little mole under the corner of the right one. These eyes looked familiar, but he could not recall where he had seen them. After a moment, the man said with a smile, "We've met before, around ten years ago".

After a couple of seconds, Isaiah was finally able to recognize him. The man was Izumi's brother, Arata. They had met ten years ago, but back then Arata had been just nine. He had grown up to have the same aura as his sister. Arata had come to Hong Kong for the summer to visit his girlfriend.

"How are you?" Arata asked. "Do you have a girlfriend? Are you married?"

"I'm married," he said. "My wife is sleeping upstairs in our apartment right now."

Arata looked up at his apartment building; it was ninety-seven stories high. "Hong Kong is so different from Tokyo," Arata said. "I wish I had more time here, but I'll be leaving soon."

"Is this your first time here?"

"Yes, I always wanted to come. My sister told me it was a place worth visiting, but I never bothered to visit until I met this girl. Maybe it's because Hong Kong is so close. When I travel, I always like to go somewhere far, away from big cities." Arata smiled.

After a short silence, and a deep breath, Isaiah finally asked, "So. How's your sister, by the way?"

Arata smiled again, looked down at his espresso, and stirred it a little before taking out a cigarette. Just before Arata could take out his lighter, Isaiah lit it for him with a match. Arata gave him another smile. This time the smile was a little less genuine. Arata then took a deep breath and told him that his sister had died last month.

"She was in a car accident, and that was it. It was fast. She didn't suffer at all."

Isaiah stared with the blank face of a shadow. She was not dead. He was almost sure that it wasn't true, yet he had no proof — nor did he have a choice but to believe what her brother was telling him. From the look on Arata's face, he could tell that Arata didn't think that he was convinced either.

Before he left, Arata asked him, "Isaiah, do you know what Izumi's name meant?" Isaiah shook his head.

"Izumi means 'spring' in Japanese, which also means the 'source of water' ..."

The manager came over with the bill. He knew Isaiah, and would always give him a discount.

"It comes to $44.30, Isaiah. On credit card?"

Isaiah paid the bill. He then asked the departing Arata for a cigarette, but he didn't smoke it. Instead, he left it on the edge of the table and slowly let it burn...

He never knew if Izumi had been planning on going to Australia or not, nor did he ask her brother. None of that mattered to him anymore. He thought about their promise, and about her. He wondered whether she was really gone, or if she had just sent her brother to see if he was married before deciding whether or not she should go to the caves. Perhaps she had simply decided that letting him believe she had died would be better than presenting him with the realities of her life. But again, none of that mattered. In society, reality and truth were never the same thing, anyway.

He thought about her outside and her inside. He thought about what it might be like to see her soul, but what did it mean? He reckoned that there should be something between her inside and her soul. Before the soul, there should be life — so that if you took away Izumi, inside you'd see life itself. If she were really dead, it'd be a life that was once lived, that had once existed. This would mean that it was a life that was once true, and that had been at the same time part of reality — actual physical reality. During her existence, he had had the fortune to meet her, to experience some of her life, and to live some part of the true reality with her. Wouldn't at least that much always be true? But that place had been swept away by time itself, to somewhere so far away that he would never be able to go back.

On his way up, he saw her brother leaving with a woman through the glass doors of the lift. It might have been his girlfriend.

He returned to his apartment, poured another scotch, and stood on his balcony. He checked the time, but for some reason his watch had stopped moving at precisely 20:47. He was sure that it was now much later than that. Maybe the battery had died. But why did it matter? Time was something marked with a system created by men; that was the only reason why time was represented by numbers. In that sense, numbers were outside of time. Then what would happen, if you took away the outside? If there were no system for telling time, what would differentiate past from present? Time would start when life started, and end when life ended. In that sense, time was just a metaphor for life.

Take away the truth, and time would be stopped at 20:47. If time was a metaphor for life, then from that point onwards all that would be left would be the soul.

From that night on, he lived with a blank face and did his job. At night he would return to his apartment. When he saw his neighbours he would greet them with a nod. He did well at work, maybe even better than ever. But since that night, all of his emotions had been swept to a place very far away. Now he would wake up in the middle of the night and find himself staring across the Hong Kong harbor as the lights turn off, one after another. One night he came back home from work and his wife was nowhere to be found. He searched the apartment and called her: invalid number.

Without longing, there is nothing to return to.

He looked at his watch and the time read 20:47. He was sure that it was much later than that.

6

AN UNCOMPLICATED WHITENESS BY BENJAMIN HERTWIG

A week after moving to Vancouver, I tell my partner I'm worried that our relationship will deteriorate into long evenings where I inform her of the amazing things I just missed on free Craigslist: the antique radio, the oak bookcase, the wooden canoe, the cassette tape collection. I don't have a place to store these things yet, but I'll eventually have a room to call my own.

My first few weeks in Vancouver, and I'm still looking for a place to live. Craigslist leads me to an intersection in East Van. A man is standing in front of a run-down two story apartment, drinking a beer.

"Anything for rent in here?" I ask. The man smiles.

"I think so," he says. "Come talk to the owner."

We walk into the building's basement. A large stuffed owl stares at me from the owner's work desk. There are many old tools and unfamiliar smells. The owner, white hair and clean-shaven, walks over to an old locker, pulls out a glass bottle. He takes a drink and stares at me too. We walk out onto the street.

"What about that room?" I say, pointing to a window.

"Not for rent," he says.

The room is inaccessible. He explains how he dry-walled over the door when the old building manager died and hasn't been in since—

hasn't had time. Dead potted plants still rest on windowsills, only visible from the street-side windows. A plastic Vancouver Canucks Memorial water bottle. A Newfoundland flag. A porcelain German shepherd. We walk up to the second story. All of the other rooms are more than I'd like to pay or are being renovated. He gives me his phone number, says he'll let me know if anything becomes available. He continues drinking as we walk back downstairs. "A lot of white people left the neighbourhood," he says. "Others moved in. Not good." He pauses. "I knew a hard-working Asian" he says. "He was good. I'd let him rent here." We walk outside. "I'm not a bad man," he says to me. He says it more than once. He stoops in his car and drives off.

I eventually find a bedroom in a musty old Strathcona house, one of the oldest neighbourhoods in Vancouver. The trees grow high above the street and the sidewalks are busy. English is not the most common language. I'm a five-minute walk from fruit and vegetable sellers in Chinatown, just off East Hastings, close to the mural of Lao Tzu. In 2015 the mural was defaced with the word "moron". In the same part of town, a different mural of five Chinese-Canadians on a park bench was similarly defaced. I spend an afternoon on the corner of Gore and East Pender, staring up at the mural. I walk into the corner store across from the mural. Through the open door, the store keeper has a clear view of the wall. I ask her about it. "Soon no more," she says. "Big apartment." She smiles and shrugs. I slowly walk back home.

The man who lived in the house before me took all the furniture when he left. The living room had a TV, a TV stand, and a couch that needed to be thrown out — that was pretty much it. I acquire a free couch off a woman on Craigslist, a desk off a man in Burnaby, plants from a student in Yaletown. I buy a dresser from a man just off Commercial Drive. He's driving an old eighties pick-up truck — boxy with horizontal stripes running down the side. We pull off the dresser together and walk towards my house.

"What an ass," he says about the girl walking in front of us. I'm not sure she's an adult. "I'd love to drop this load on her," he says with a sneer. He speaks like a sneer looks and assumes an easy familiarity. We are both male and white — maybe, like Trump with Billy Bush,he assumes comradery on that basis. Maybe my silence means that he's right.

"It's okay here on the porch right?" I say yes. I'm glad when he leaves. I start my summer class at UBC. Every day I'm taking the number 14 bus, up and down East Hastings, on the way to school. Every day I pass the downtown community garden and tent city. On the fence of the community garden, there is a wooden sign in the shape of an eagle feather — *Culture Saves Lives.* In the window of one of the apartment buildings behind the community garden, there is a large confederate flag. I wonder about the owner of the flag. Who he is, what he's trying to accomplish.

I've been in Strathcona for a while now. The arugula seed I brought from the prairies has started to sprout. I recognize some of the bottle pickers. They recognize me. The once-strange scratching from inside the roof is now just the busy, old squirrel that hops between trees during the day and squeezes between rafters at night. It hasn't started raining yet — I'm starting to feel a sense of safety and belonging.

The third month in Vancouver and my girlfriend sits in her bedroom while her housemate's boyfriend rages about traffic and the *stupid chink drivers.* Across the city, my housemates and I are sitting on our front porch when a woman screams from the alley. We run over.

"Asshole," she yells, gathering her scattered purse and walking away. The attacker is far away and running, his coat blending in with the alley.

My partner and I attend *Dirty Knees*, an art exhibition of hybridized female, Asian identity, and after, we go out for food. I ask my partner what ethnicity she thinks the server is. We get into an argument. I feel as though my partner, who is herself Asian, is subtly accusing me of racism. I'm embarrassed. *I'm just curious*, I say. *What's wrong with that?*

White fragility is a concept I'm exposed to in Vancouver: the proclivity for white people to get defensive when questioned about their understanding of race. It makes sense to me now. But it didn't at the restaurant. I was still angry. *Those people* — the landlord, the Craigslist man, the owner of the confederate flag, the roommate's boyfriend — *they* are the racists, I say to myself.

Our argument continues to bother me: I don't think of myself as racist. I reflect on recent Craigslist interactions. Whenever I've been arranging a free furniture pick-up and heard someone well-spoken and without accent on the phone, I've always assumed the speaker was white. And every time I've gone to pick something up, the well- spoken, accent-less woman or man has *not* been white. The man in Burnaby who gave me the free antique roll-top desk was from India, the woman with the orange, seventies couch was Chinese.

I walk back to the mural. It's raining today. I sit down under a store awning and ask Lao Tzu what ethnicity he is. He says he was born far from here. I tell him he is a hard-working Asian, that I'd let him rent a room in my apartment building. He says nothing. A man runs down the street and knocks Lao Tzu off the bull. Lao Tzu is on his hands and knees, gathering his scattered belongings. Another man rides past on a bicycle, yells *stupid chink*, rings his bell and keeps pedaling.

In Vancouver, there are rooms within rooms, dry-walled over, visible only from the outside. Between the compartments I've made in my mind, the walls that separate me from those people, the racists, there is a place where I remain one myself. The social forces that lead me to wonder about a person's ethnicity before their personhood, the whiteness as default position — these are the same social forces that create *those chinks*, the Confederate flag, the Indigenous woman in the alley gathering her scattered possessions, the defaced and disappearing murals. In the upper-left corner of the Lao Tzu mural, there is a quotation: "It takes knowledge to understand others, but it needs a clear mind to know oneself. It takes strength to surpass others, but it requires a strong will to surpass oneself."

My partner and I are still figuring out how to live into our different experiences of race, and I'm still learning how to live in a new city. As a child I lived an uncomplicated whiteness, mostly surrounded by people who looked and spoke like me. Being in a new environment has forced me to examine the ways I perceive that whiteness in relation to the world around me, a world where people of colour are more aware of the implications than I am. My partner has helped me learn that being racist doesn't mean you are evil: it means you have work to do.

The last time I walked past the Lao Tzu mural, the construction frames had risen to his chest.

7

TWO POEMS BY HELEN TRAN

HOI AN

rooms with windows
opening to beauty
the reclining sunset, the sandy moon
the swilling harbor, the bright boats
these are the sterile rooms
where people leave no stories
where my sweat leaves no trace
where tear stains wash easily
out of the pillows
these are rooms that look out
on beaches where old women still cross
with bamboo yokes pulling their livelihoods:
quail eggs, small and warm in my hand
less than a penny each.

DA LAT FAMILY GARDEN, 1976

the banana trees are thriving,
despite the bombing the week before
unlike the rest of the house
where some children peep through
the bulletholes in the wall
the youngest is crying on the front step
where their dog used to sleep
while the rest are giggling
as the adults slowly thread the bananas
with hot chilis — little fire missiles,
meant for the monkeys that lately
have decided to visit where else would they find
food, one child asks, when the jungle
is burning all the time,
and one of the elders makes an angry noise,
reminding all of how the beasts tore apart
with their innocent human hands
the trees, the flowers, the shadows in the garden,
everything except
the new red, yellow-starred flag hanging
on the fence.

8

THREE MICROAGGRESSIONS BY JF GARRARD

Not Blonde

For some reason, America expected her skin to turn lily-white, her body to blossom into perfect proportions and her hair to turn blonde, when she turned sixteen. She poked her brown belly, lamented over her stringy black hair. Tears welled up in her hazel eyes. She took out her dog-eared teenage romance book, tore it into pieces, and flushed it down the toilet.

Can't Grow Roots

"Where are you from?" the professor asked Ned in front of the class.

"Er, Houston..."

"No, you're not," the professor shook his head and continued his interrogation. "Where are you really from?"

Face

All the stories must be great, fantastical and magical! No one can know the truth about how difficult it is in the new country, or we will be laughed at, mocked and ridiculed for dreaming of a new life away from our motherland. We must put on our masks and no matter how difficult, deny our hardships so that the next generation can innocently bask in the glory of their own success without the outsiders knowing our burdens.

9

CARRYING THE SOUL BACK HOME BY ZENG XIAOWEN

TRANSLATED BY ALISON BAILEY

The trip home is always long.

Setting off from Toronto on a thirteen-hour flight followed by a two-hour bus ride, I finally arrived at a small town in the Central Plain of China. I was physically exhausted but even more mentally fatigued by the anticipation of a special reunion. When I went through the front door of the family home I came face to face with a photo of my father in his prime, the thick black hair a testament to his youth, the straight nose indicative of his character, and the bright, clear, sincere gaze piercing through the thick dust of months and years. Below the photo was everything he had left to me: approximately 3,000 books. They stood in bookcases made of different materials, but at attention, as if waiting for my arrival. In that one glance it was as if all the windows in that room had suddenly crashed open and a strong wind that had crossed the oceans lashed at the tree of my heart and shook down wounded fruit all across the ground.

The last time that I returned home was over a year ago when my father, having gone through all kinds of treatments, was still bravely pitting himself against lung cancer. Who would have guessed that less than two months after I left he finally broke his halberd and buried it in the sand in surrender before the god of death? And I, who lived over

10,000 kilometers away, would be reminded of him almost every day by tiny details that seemed to bear no obvious connection to him. I would look up at the sun hanging in a clear azure sky, think that he would never again feel the warmth of sunlight, and then my tears would fall. Or there would be news on the TV of a stranger's death, making me feel sad for the children of someone I had never met, because I knew only too well the pain of losing someone close. Those wounds had been wrapped carelessly in the white gauze of time, but how could I avoid my heart breaking now as I faced my father's image and his book collection?

My father's photo was in black and white, taken in the 1950s. He had been studying Chinese literature at university then and was known for his exceptional literary talent. He was also an assistant chief editor of a student journal. He had published some short stories and had even been awarded a provincial literary prize. Not long after, however, because he had told the truth in commenting that "ordinary people don't have enough grain to eat", his words were declared "Rightist". After graduating, he volunteered to go to a small town in the Northeast to teach language at middle school. It was as if Fate's cold finger had flicked lightly through the secret ledgers and inscribed his name in the shadowy official files, unwilling to release him from torment for the next twenty years. He maintained his deep abiding love for writing and, relying on a rich foundation of classical learning, in his spare time had translated into modern Chinese many classical language texts such as statesman Su Dongpo's "Random Sayings of Master Ai". He sent them to the famous historian Mr. Wu Han, receiving accolades and recommendations for his work. When the Cultural Revolution began in 1966, Mr. Wu Han suffered terrible persecution and my father, because of his correspondence with him, was labeled a "member of the Black Gang". Red Guards shaved my father's hair in the"yin-yang" pattern, and tried him before a citywide rally. They hung a big blackboard around his neck, and then paraded him through the streets standing in an open truck. His newly published short story collection was dispatched back to the printer's and pulped, along with his smashed literary dreams. The day I was born he had been locked in the "cow shed" to "reflect on his crimes." He asked one of the guards to take a note to my mother on which he had written the name he had chosen for me: Xiaowen — profound literary discernment — thereby entrusting his literary dreams to me.

I slowly passed my hand along row after row of books, their spines still seeming to hold on to my father's warmth. In the 1960s, my father had been sent off to a tiny remote mountain village in the Northeast to do "reform through labour", carrying me with him on his back to be raised by a peasant family. A year later, he carried me on his back again to the city, sending me to stay at my maternal grandmother's. His back was my childhood cradle. On the farm he planted crops and drove an ox-drawn cart, only returning home to the city seven years later, but still deprived of the right to teach and only able to do some odd jobs in the school's factory. In the summer of 1976, because he came under suspicion in the movement to oppose the tendency to "Rehabilitate the Case for Rightists," he was unjustly sent to prison, nearly being sentenced to death. During the time he was in prison, I was shunned by neighbours and insulted by my classmates, hiding alone in a small room reading his collection of books, using the lamplight of literature to stave off life's darkness.

Over the last twenty years, whenever I phoned home from abroad, my father would enthusiastically report on the new books he had bought, even going into detail of which bookshop in which town and how much of a discount he had obtained. Books and alcohol — those were his life's obsessions. Throughout his life he teetered between the clarity of books and the haze of drink. It is only now that I have come to realize that it was due to the mental anguish caused by a series of tragic experiences that he looked to alcohol for escape; but perhaps only books served as the vessel for him to cross the bitter sea.

I decided to select a few boxes worth of my father's collection to be shipped to Canada. Those books had accompanied my father as he moved from place to place and would now accompany me on a new journey. Without my father, home would lose the deep significance it had once held. All I could do was to take some books with me, preserving a life's memories.

And yet how painful and difficult this process of selection was!

On opening each volume the countless creative spirits of the original Chinese characters created by Cang Jie would jump out at me and for a split second the world would become something extraordinary. When I returned home in 2005 I took back with me the first 20 volumes of the *Twenty-four Histories*, and this time I packed up the remaining 46 volumes in cartons, thereby ensuring I at least had the complete history. My father had said that everyone should study and respect history. I found Romain Rolland's *Jean-Christophe.* Many years ago when I set out on the tough road of studying for a master's degree in world literature my father began collecting foreign literary works. He knew that *Jean-Christophe* was my favourite and bought three different translations of it all at once. One sentence has always been an inspiration to me: "I have struggled; I have suffered; I have erred; I have created.[1]"

I saw several of the books I had written. Those days when I had relied on the warmth of the written word in the cold winters of a foreign land once again came walking towards me on snow in my memory. After I had published my first book my father enthusiastically bought a hundred copies which he gave to his old classmates, as if announcing to them that I had inherited his reverence for literature and great love for writing — his literary dream like a phoenix rising from the ashes.

I slowly took down two plainly bound handbooks on classical Chinese for the national university entrance exams that my father had written. A few years ago, when he knew he had an incurable disease, he had ignored his family's objections and grabbed hold of every spare moment to write. He had been a teacher for nearly half a century and committed himself to passing on his experience of teaching middle school Chinese to a new generation. He did not know how to use a computer, so he wrote everything by hand. After he had written the first draft he proofread it five times. I could not imagine how he could carry on working while undergoing chemotherapy and radiation. These two books were no more than 600 pages in all, but the abundant strength of his willpower made them weigh as heavy as a ton as I held them in my hand — from this time on I would never again dare to think of giving up while writing.

My gaze fell on a collection of Pushkin's poetry. Opening the cover was like opening up the silver screen of the years, once again finding myself in a familiar landscape. Many years ago my father had stood in a small room with bare walls, reciting "Exegi Monumentum" with great emotion:

**Exegi Monumentum, By A.S. Pushkin.
Translated by A.Z. Foreman**

I've raised a monument not made by human hands.
The public path to it cannot be overgrown.
With insubmissive head far loftier it stands
Than Alexander's columned stone.
No, I shall not all die. My soul in hallowed berth
Of art shall brave decay and from my dust take wing, And I shall be renowned whilst on this mortal earth
Even one poet lives to sing.

My father never became a well-known poet or writer, but he was admired and loved by legions of good friends and students, and I somehow return again and again to recording chapter after chapter of his life, so that his life history now occupies every corner of my world. These memories are stacked up in our hearts to form his Exegi Monumentum.

Several months later, when my father's books had arrived at my house in Toronto, I was unable to sort them out immediately — not for any physical barrier, but because of a mental one. The boxes of books seemed to be filled with a fog of anguish that would cover my heart like a pall if I opened them. Facing a personal unalloyed spiritual emptiness, all I could do was to sit at my desk and write. My father had many regrets on the eve of his passing, one of them being that he would not be able to read more of my works. If only I were to write, his life would continue. And although the stories I write have no connection to his own experience, in my thoughts he is always my first reader.

I commissioned someone to make me an oak bookcase fitted with lights and finally tidily arranged my father's books on the shelves, as reverentially as if performing a religious rite. My father and I were living in completely different realms, and yet his comments and fingerprints in the books were still in my world. In legends, it is said that a shaman can carry the soul of the departed back home to communicate with the living. These books were like countless shamans pulling me into an endlessly unfolding dialogue with my father, so that in the midst of the hubbub of this chaotic world I had a tiny bit of serenity.

I live in a foreign country where Chinese is not the primary language, ceaselessly writing in my spare time, carving out a clear spiritual pool where the roots of my soul can plant themselves and my deep-seated feelings can spread out on the water like lotus flowers all year round. Perhaps I, along with other writers living abroad, carry on my back the legacy of Chinese culture as we endlessly walk along the road to our spiritual home, raising a"monument not made by human hands", using words to "awaken people's noble feelings."

---

[1] Rolland, Romain, Jean Christophe: Journey's End, Dodo Collections, 2015

10

PRITONG ISDA BY AILEEN SANTOS

Pritong isda smells foreign to my friends. Scales flaked off with a cleaver, gutted to its eyeballs, fried in a pan with rice until the smells — residual oil dripping off crispy hardened morsels, used the night before to fry lumpia, fried chicken, egg — land on people's clothing, in their hair, on their skin, rice pouring from within.

In my late teens, I refused to enter my house if my grandma was frying anything. The smell dirtied the air, made me feel like a squatter in the slums, or a back alley dumpster filled with day-old scraps. It wasn't a privileged smell, like lavender or citrus or Pine Sol sold on shelves in stores; it wasn't a white people smell.

But still, when I knew I was going nowhere where I needed to pass or fit in, I'd get into my *pang-bahay*, house clothing of shorts and an oversized T-shirt, sit at the table and tear up the fish with my bare, impatient hands. I'd scoop up the rice, thumb kissing fingers, cradle a gluten ball that I'd stuff into my mouth with pieces of fish that lazily hung out. I'd sit with my grandma, chattering away, fried tilapia swimming in vinegar, soya sauce, tiny garlic bits and my saliva. My taste buds would jump up like *Tinikling* where your feet would get chopped off if you weren't careful or looking. The pungent acidity would move up into my nostrils, causing my eyes to water and my ears to ring. Tiny bones threatened to choke me as I stuffed it all down gluttonously. I sat and listened to her, speaking in Tagalog, tasting home, feeling full.

My grandma died a few years ago. I married a Canadian. I moved to a place where I am the only spot of colour in a sea of white picket fences. My kids prefer cereal, toast and McDonald's, forks and knives and spoons. They've never seen me eat with my hands or see the *pritong isda* and I feel barren, lonely, something missing here. I sit staring at whitewash walls, granite counters, empty smells that leave a hole. My kids barrel in, ask for Wonder Bread, pasta, and I think — I wish I paid more attention to my grandma and her fish.

11

THE DIKE BY CAROUSEL CALVO

The day Luis left for Vancouver was the same day my mother gave birth to my younger brother. Both arrival and departure were unwanted. At the well, as I washed rags full of blood and shit, Luis had told me everything will be as before. This time, his promise was a burden I didn't want to carry. In my mind's eye were a multitude of women carrying the weight of unfulfilled promises throughout their lifetime. I trembled at the thought of their shared destinies. Across from me, Manang Marta's hands were white and cracked from using too much chlorine when washing clothes. Her back did not straighten from the many years scrubbing the cement floor of her tiny house. With her small store, she supported three grown sons who stole money from the cash box and drank the liquor from her own stock. I looked down at the soiled clothes and saw my mother's legs wide open, waiting for the child to come out. Blood and water on the bamboo floor. When my little brother came out, he was so small, already a resigned look on his face. I looked at the path where Luis disappeared, wanting to leave as much as he wanted to stay. He was stupid for thinking that there was something to stay behind for. What he told me echoed all around me. He had said, with his usual cherry optimism, "I'll get there then I'll come back right after. Promise." We were behind the stacks of empty crates of Red Horse beer so

Manang Marta couldn't hear us. I memorized his face, his hair, his hands on my forearm. The small scar on the side of his left eyebrow, when he jumped from the dike to the sea bed, a submerged branch struck him when he stumbled. He tried to circle me in his arms but I stepped back. "You should go. You'll be late," I said. There was confusion in his eyes but I had nothing else to say so I headed back to Manang Marta and squatted next to her to rinse the blood and shit from my mother's clothes.

During siesta, I went to the end of the dike where the bangkas were moored and hid myself inside a tarp draped over empty fishing baskets. I then allowed myself to believe that in a few hours, Luis would be waiting for me on the bridge that connected my house to the dike, writing English words on the concrete floor with the chalk he always carried.

OUR HOUSE
OUR GARDEN
ROSES ARE RED
VIOLETS ARE BLUE
I WANT TO MARRY YOU.

I'd erase the word MARRY, thinking that I didn't want to be married because all I would do is have children and more children and get sad when most of them died. Like Mama, I would cry every All Soul's Day. What I had always told Luis was, "just because we are always together doesn't mean that we will end up together." He'd laugh and then pull me down to sit next to him and sang that song he always sang, his voice so much like the scratched noises a karaoke machine makes when it stopped working. And in that moment, the song was mine, the feeling was mine, the sea wind was mine, the world was ours.

When I left my sanctuary, the dike was still the tall, rough sentry that it was, and the houses crowded behind its walls were the same stilt houses as yesterday and the months and years before. Despite typhoons and tropical storms, people had built their homes the same way they'd always built them. They had never learned to move away. They had never told the typhoons, the blackened sea bed, the capricious sea that they have had enough. They should have packed their bags, destroyed their stilt houses, and moved far away. To move, just move. I turned my back on them and looked towards the horizon.

My moment of clarity drove me to ask Manang Marta if she knew of a place where I could work. Carlo, her eldest son, snored on the bamboo bench. He scratched his balls inside his basketball shorts. He reminded me of the pig Manang Marta raised last year. The same look of contentment when it settled in the wet mud in the afternoon heat. From where I stood, he smelled of rum.

"What do you need work for? How about school? Who's going to help with... the little baby? What with your Mama not getting out of bed."

I understood her nosiness. Everyone in the barangay shared every bit of good and bad luck. Everyone knew who had dysentery, who needed help mending fishing nets, who fucked which neighbour and showed up pregnant and hiding it. I resented her inquiries. I wanted something for myself.

I gave her a reason she understood, "Papa's not home. He's gone again."

"Does your mother know?"

"Yes." I lied. Her stare left me uncomfortable but I held my gaze.

"I know a girl who works for a rich Intsik. They might need a tindera at their warehouse in Carcar."

"Can you tell her that I would like to work for them? That I can start right away?"

"Don't you want to finish school?"

"The public school has night classes."

"Madre Dios, you want to get raped?!" Manang Marta woke up Carlo with her scream.

"Who's getting raped?" Carlo leered at me from his reclined position.

"Mind your own business," I said.

"Can you please get up? Get up and wash the dishes." Manang

Marta smacked Carlo's bare shoulders. It left a red imprint that faded in seconds.

"I'm hungry."

"You and your brothers ..."

"Will you shut up! Nag. Nag. Nag. All you do is nag. Hand me twenty pesos. I'm going to buy food at the carinderia." He got up and scratched his balls again. This time he looked at me. "Do you want to come with me, pretty Rowena? Luis isn't here to walk you around anymore."

"Stop talking," Manang Marta said.

"Ha! I bet a thousand pesos he'll forget he was ever born here. He'll forget how pretty Rowena is pining for him."

"Manang, just tell me when you hear from the girl." As I was about to leave, Carlo snaked his hands inside Manang Marta's long apron, snatching bills; he left her screaming of how much she suffered.

When I arrived home, Berto and Miguel were playing on the dike. Boys with snot and dirt on their small faces. Their small bellies protruding. They had been scavenging for garbage in the sea bed: broken toys, empty bottles, unopened containers. I told them to be careful but the wind snatched my words. The air tasted of rain. The bridge connecting my family's stilt house to the dike swayed rhythmically. I told the boys to pack the fishing nets before the deluge. They nodded their heads before hammering open a tin box with a big rock. Once inside the small house, my mother barely looked at me. Her face was slack and dehydrated, a dusting of dandruff coating her long hair. I tidied as much as I could without waking the baby sleeping in his cardboard box.

"I got a job so I'm switching to night school." My mother applied Vicks VapoRub on her chest and neck. The bowl of lugaw on the table left untouched. "I'll walk home with Clara. Her boyfriend picks her up from school."

"No," she said. The skin on her upper arms jiggled when she rubbed vigorously.

"Ma, who's going to feed the family?"

The baby mewled as the strong sea wind blew through the closed window. Without answering, my mother closed her eyes and covered herself with a thin blanket.

ꕥ

While Clara waited for me outside my classroom door, Hector and Paul boxed her into a corner. They thought they looked cool with their hair slick with gel and cigarettes dangling behind their ears. I knew Hector wanted to touch Clara's hair, to pull down the red scrunchy holding it in place. When Clara's hair was down her back, she looked like a hair model from a Sunsilk Shampoo commercial.

"Can you please..." Clara said.

"Of course you can pleaassse..." Paul said.

Clara moved to the right and Hector blocked her.

"Don't you have something better to do?" Clara tilted her head up since Paul had the height of PBA basketball player. He sometimes played for the varsity team.

"Rowena, I'll meet you outside the school gate. Jomar is waiting already." Clara turned around in a huff, her ponytail swinging angrily.

With opportunity, Hector grabbed the scrunchy. As Clara's hair cascaded down her back in ebony waves, Paul laughed while Hector bounced the scrunchy up and down his hand. Clara shook, maybe from anger, maybe from something else. I got to her as fast as I could, I kicked Paul's shin and punched Hector's shoulder. Clara picked up her scrunchy when it dropped on the floor.

"Puta! Get the fuck away from her!"

"Kayat! That hurt, Wang." Hector rubbed his shoulder while Paul glared at me from three feet away.

"I'm going to do more than that if you don't leave right now." It was 10:30 P.M. and in seven hours I had to be up to bathe and change Berto and Miguel so they could stay at Manang Marta's. I had to be at Mr. Yang's warehouse by eight.

"You okay?" Clara pulled her hair into a tight bun, the scrunchy a crown on her head again. "Did they touch you?" I leaned in to whisper.

"Let's just get out of here." She adjusted her pristine white school blouse, making sure the checkered red and green ribbon was where it should be. I shouldered my own school bag and left with her. We heard catcalls in our wake.

Jomar, Clara's boyfriend, was twenty, four years older, and a college graduate with an engineering degree. She boasted about it to anyone who listened. "Not like the palahubogs at the corner store," she'd say. Jomar had dimples, Intsik eyes, and hair parted in the middle like the idol Keempee de Leon. He always wore Converse high-top shoes, as if rubber slippers weren't good enough anymore. He carried The Republic: just carried it around, never reading it. When Clara had a peek, she didn't understand any of the words. It was in English but not in English sometimes. There were words like polis which she thought was about the policia. "Who wants to read about the police when they never help unless there was cash involved," she said. She once nagged Jomar to carry his engineering study book instead so he could finally pass the board exam. To shut her up, Jomar twirled her around until she was dizzy and laughing. They were happy, as much as poverty allowed them to be. I looked at them and wondered how long before Clara had a child. They'd probably marry before she graduates from high school. He'd give up on being an engineer. His parents would be disappointed and, in a few years, he'd take over his father's carpentry shop. They'd have five or six children, probably two miscarriages, and by the time Clara's thirty she'd have that look in her eyes. The same as my mother's.

Jomar usually waited next to the fish ball vendor's store. Sometimes he'd be talking with a group of students. Other times, he'd be alone, reading the daily newspaper. If he could get his hands on an English paper, he'd read that instead. Tonight he was reading *The Philippine Inquirer* with his legs stretched out in front of him. Already the store was full of students dipping their thin sticks into deep fried snacks. Their chatter was loud, attracting stray dogs, sniffing around khaki pants and plaid skirts. As I exited the school, the gate keeper, Opaw— so named for his shiny bald head — gestured at me to come near him. I flipped him the bird. Up ahead, Clara dashed out, her crown of hair bobbing then finally coming undone. The scrunchy lay forgotten on the side of the road. Jomar looked up from his reading to find her crying in front of him.

"What's wrong? What happened? Are you hurt?" He wrapped his arms around Clara and looked at me accusingly. Since Jomar could not go inside school grounds, he relied on me to keep Clara safe. As a concession, I picked up the forgotten scrunchy off the street and offered it to him. When he didn't take it, I slipped it inside my bag.

Opaw knew he was the shit. And everybody understood this. He was a conspicuous pervert. He leered and made smarmy gestures to students he fancied, boys and girls alike. He touched their bottoms, sometimes pinched their waist, and always fondled their genitals. When he tried to grope my ass, I slapped him but that only made him open his mouth and stick his tongue out from between his missing front teeth. He liked Jomar, liked the way he smelled and how he looked so much like the Keempee de Leon. Maybe Opaw envied Jomar's hair. Who knew. But as soon as Jomar asked him if he could pick up Clara inside school grounds, Opaw lunged towards Jomar's penis. It was no surprise when Jomar beat the bald man to the ground. Blood gushed from cuts above his right eyebrow and the bridge of his flat nose. Jomar told the gatekeeper that he would report him to the barangay captain. Opaw laughed. He laughed so hard that he swallowed blood trickling down from his wounds, "He's my cousin, you fool! Unless you suck my cock, you're not stepping foot inside."

Clara sobbed until Jomar's shirt was wet. I was certain that he was going to do something incredibly stupid soon.

"Was it Hector and Paul again?" he asked me.

"Why do you ask if you already know the answer?" I wanted to go home and do my homework and sleep for at least 5 hours. I was an unwanted third person in their couple universe but walking with them kept me safe from palahubogs who were drunk from rum and high on *shabu*.

"You have to stop working and go back to school in the morning. I know we can convince your mom," he said.

"She'll say the same thing, you know she will." Below the streetlight, they looked more like father and daughter than two lovers.

"I'm going to ask again. I'll make sure she understands." I walked slowly ahead.

Unemployed since he failed the board exam twice, Jomar was unable to move to the city. He had a useless college degree that he couldn't use in a village where most houses were built out of corrugated steel and stolen plywood and bamboo. Those who could afford to build concrete houses on solid land hired people with board certified engineering degrees so their castles wouldn't topple on them at the first gust of a tropical storm. The little money his mother gave him for allowance wasn't enough to pay for extra expenses, like transferring Clara to a daytime high school. When they finally caught up to me, their arms were around each other as if holding off the disappointments of the world.

12

FROM WHOM THE MAPLE LEAVES TURN RED BY ANNA WANG YUAN

Although I always loved listening to the radio while driving, I never totally paid attention to what was on. But one BC Day when I was passing 12th Street, a song came on that demanded my full attention.

Beautiful, beautiful, British Columbia..., it began.

The melody embraced me. Proud, yet unassuming. I cranked up the volume, and let it take me on a euphoric trip, even though I only half understood the lyrics. But the opening was the only line I unquestioningly understood.

I tried to find out what the song was for years. My options for finding out were limited since I only knew a few people who spoke English as their first language. I'd fumble through singing the one line I knew, but they all shook their heads. They'd ask me to go on, but by then the melody had already vanished into thin air. All except that one line.

Some years later, Laoxin and I walked into the Immigration, Refugees and Citizenship Canada office on Hornby Street. We were there to pick up my husband's second Maple Leaf Card.

He handed his red notice to a security guard standing behind a desk in a deep recessed area. Red meant "Final". Anyone with a red notice who didn't come get their card at this point might as well never come back.

Once inside, Laoxin and I waited under a giant red maple leaf pained on a snow-white wall. We had a view of station one, where an officer sat behind the desk sorting papers. She looked up and called out a long name, which sent the other side of the hall into a state of disarray until an elderly woman in a wheelchair was pushed over by a heavily bearded man who appeared to be her husband. The officer remarked on the old woman's spryness, and asked what her secret was. The husband interpreted and after getting her answer, relayed something I couldn't hear back to the interviewer. "You're so lucky!" the interviewer exclaimed.

She was so easygoing! I nudged Laoxin and pointed to the female officer's station. "I hope we'll be interviewed by her," I said.

He didn't look nearly as relieved as me. "Looks like station three isn't so lucky... can you hear anything?"

The interviewee in station three was a middle-aged East Asian woman. She sat up extremely straight. It was the farthest station from where we were sitting, so I couldn't hear a single word. Still, I could at least tell that the story playing out was much less celebratory.

Back at station one, the old couple had left, and another name was called. A middle-aged Asian man and his son came forward. As they sat, the interviewer spoke to the son sternly. "Listen," she began. She coldly stated that any questions she might ask needed to be directly translated to the applicant, and he was to interpret his father's answer, but at no time was he to answer for him. It was a fair request, but I could already see where this was headed.

The man was from mainland China, and was a so-called Tai Kong Ren. An "astronaut": immigrants who split their time between China and North America. Most "astronauts" have problems fulfilling their residency obligations. Some of them go as far as to fake their records when they try to renew their Maple Leaf Cards.

The interviewer asked for the man's passport. He handed it to her with both hands and she carefully checked every page. China's border officers stamped every passport upon entry and exit, making it easy to track how often and for how long he was back in China.

It seemed that his record was all right. She asked him to sign something. But after he handed the signed document back to her, she didn't stand and congratulate him as she did the old lady. Instead, she coldly pushed the envelope across the desk and raised her voice as if teaching him a lesson: "If you guys really want to call Canada home..."

I couldn't hear the rest of the sentence.

My husband is an "astronaut" too.

He ran a chain of fast food restaurants in China. You may wonder why it was so difficult for him to give up his business back home. Or, if his business was so indispensable, why on earth did he want to immigrate to Canada in the first place? But in the beginning, we were so confident that things would be different — that we'd be different in Canada.

Several years ago the four of us — myself, Laoxin, and my children embarked upon a seven-day trip to Vancouver. We had our immigration papers stamped and applied for Social Insurance Numbers. Reality sank in: we were permanent residents of Canada. We needed to consider when to move permanently. Were we going before the New Year or Chinese New Year? Were we moving to Vancouver or Toronto? With these questions in mind, we spent our days in Vancouver as tourists with a focus on culinary discovery.

Our culinary journey took us through from fine dining restaurants like The Keg Steakhouse and Steveston Seafood House, as well as casual eateries like White Spot and Denny's, and, last but not least, Canadian fast food staples like Tim Hortons.

One day, the kids were fed up with having to behave in restaurants so we drove to Stanley Park. We wandered along the seawall and forest trails before I realized that we'd lost our way. For a moment, I panicked because Stanley Park is a thousand acres of primitive forests peppered with man-made structures here and there, and we hadn't seen any trace of people in a while. The day grew dark and there wasn't anyone in sight.

But after a few aimless turns, we stumbled across a cottage radiating a warm, merciful light. "The Fish House", read a dimly lit sign, damp with evening condensation. My guidebook said it was a renowned fine dining restaurant and one of the most difficult spots to get a reservation in Vancouver. Yet, there we were, suddenly speaking to the hostess, who, upon spotting the Lonely Planet in my hand, offered to add a table in the corner. The table faced the kitchen, so every plate of food that came out passed by our eyes and noses. It wasn't a sought-after spot for everyday customers who only wanted to enjoy their own meal, but we weren't everyday customers. To Laoxin, this was the best seat in the house. Each time that kitchen door opened, he craned his neck to see everything he could before the door swung shut.

On the plane ride back to China, Laoxin glumly admitted that his trusted ways of doing business would be no match for Canada. And then, there we were, caught in the same dilemma as every astronaut's family before us: On one side is China, a developing country in every aspect, where anyone with a little more talent or dedication than average can achieve unparalleled success. At the same time, it's a socialist/communist country by constitution, where private assets are forever at risk being confiscated without warning. On the other side, Canada, a country that for many Chinese people represents law and order, peace, stability and democracy, but is home to a market that has grown steadily for so long that it's hard for a newcomer to break into.

Just like that, our family begrudgingly joined the growing ranks of astronauts.

Five years flashed by. Laoxin stayed in Canada, 480 days too short to keep his Permanent Resident status.

In the interest of maintaining his status, I'd temporarily moved with the kids back to China after becoming a Canadian citizen. Laoxin's application to renew his card was based on the principle that the days a permanent resident spends living outside of Canada accompanying a Canadian citizen can be counted as physically present in Canada for residency purposes. It was a valid principle. Completely above-board.

But after I walked into the interview hall, I felt uneasy. We weren't truly sincere about our claims to call Canada home. We were constantly weighing the pros and cons. If I was a Canadian immigration officer, any time a Chinese applicant sat down in front of me, a warning light would go off right above their head.

For the past three years, I had been living in Beijing as an overseas Canadian Resident. When anyone asked, I always said that my move back to Beijing was just to help Laoxin get his card renewed. But that was all behind us. If he got his new card, would I really move back to Vancouver? And if I would, when?

The woman at Station Three clumsily got up before hastily leaving the hall. As she passed in front of us, her face was beet-red with a mix of dejection and anger. And then it was Laoxin's turn. Together we trudged to station three. The interviewer was a man of Asian descent. My heart sank nervously. In my experience, Asian officers, Chinese especially, were the hardest to deal with.

He pointed to the chair and asked Laoxin to sit, before asking who I was. I replied that I was his wife, and he responded that any questions he might ask needed to be directly translated to Laoxin, and I was to interpret his answer. At no time was I to answer for him.

"Sure."

He turned to his computer and typed a few commands, before staring at the screen for what seemed like an eternity. He abruptly turned from his computer, looked Laoxin straight in the eyes, and said angrily, "You think you're pretty smart, eh? You're using our system."

I was speechless, much less able to translate. He turned to me and repeated: "You're using our system."

"How?"

"Canadian immigration law does allow that the days a permanent resident lives outside of Canada accompanying a Canadian citizen to be counted as physically present in Canada, but this law is intended to be for Canadian citizens who have no choice but to leave the country for work or other official reasons. In other words, you," he pointed to me, "should be the party who works in China. He," he pointed to

Laoxin, "should be the one who stayed home to cook and watch the kids."

I was dumbfounded. This was the law in Canada? How could I have not paid closer attention when filling out the form? Was it possible that there were tiny, light-colored letters printed in the corner of the application that had escaped my attention? Just like a cigarette pack in the old days; a teeny-tiny, almost transparent line of words printed at the bottom concealing a lethal warning?

We weren't intending to "use" anything. We honestly thought that it was a good, legal way to get Laoxin a new card. It never occurred to us that we needed to worry about who was "accompanying" who. But in light of the officer's bitter explanation, I did see that we weren't entirely innocent.

I fished in my bag for a piece of paper, on which was written: Alberta Slim / Beautiful British Columbia / Canada, My Homeland. I handed it to the confused interviewer.

"For years, I've been searching for this song," I told him."Today I got here too early, and went to a second-hand bookstore to kill time. I asked the owner about the song I was searching for. Based on the lyrics I remembered, he recognized it! He didn't have it in stock, but he wrote down all the information I would need to find it online. The artist is Alberta Slim, the album is *Canada, My Homeland,* and the song is *Beautiful British Columbia*."

His glare softened. "I know you're a Canadian citizen, I don't have any doubts about you. But does your husband have any intention of actually living in Canada? What are you going to do if he can't live here for 730 days out of next five years?"

I hesitated.

He smiled. "Here's what I think he should do: He should give up his PR status right here and now, and stop wasting his time."

Maybe it is a good thing to give it up now. I thought. Suppose he gets his second card, and I move back to Vancouver in 2015. And then what? I'm destined to move once again to China in 2018 for his third card. I don't mind wandering from place to place. But what about the kids, briefly forced to move back to China when I stayed with Laoxin?

I shook off my qualms and relayed the interviewer's question to

Laoxin. I watched him nervously, hoping he wouldn't give the answer I expected.

Without missing a beat, Laoxin answered, "Of course I want to live in Canada."

He sounded so convincing.

We left the building with the envelope in Laoxin's hand. Inside was the precious Maple Leaf Card for which I'd exchanged three years of my life in Beijing. But a sadness lingered within me. Laoxin just made a promise he couldn't keep. I knew that.

Four years earlier, a gray whale made a surprise visit to False Creek. For two days and nights, audiences gathered at both banks, watching the lost creature lashing the waves back and forth before given an escort by a Vancouver police boat and a coast guard inflatable while a small flotilla of sea kayakers trailed behind.

When anyone asked, I always said that my move back to Beijing was just to help Laoxin. But if that were true, I would have made sure to follow every instruction as closely as possible. Instead, I overlooked small requirements right and left, and as a result, the process had been dragged so long as to the point where Laoxin was given a red notice. I guess a part of me still loved my life in Beijing. But why, then, did I feel such a rush of emotion as I walked out of the building and once again put my eyes at Vancouver's skyline? The whale knew the inlet wasn't its home. It was just lost. I thought of Beijing and Vancouver. Which zip code would I use forever? Or would I keep wandering on?

The middle-aged woman from station three was standing in the parking lot, smoking a cigarette feverishly. On seeing us, she forced a pained smile.

"That's discrimination back there!" She said."The hostility against us Chinese is getting worse and worse!"

I forced a sympathetic smile back to her before I hastily crept into our car.

I felt uncomfortable too, but I wouldn't call the accusation and admonition from the interviewer discrimination. He was most likely also of Chinese descent and this made him even more critical of us. He probably thought that Chinese new immigrants like us somehow averaged down the morality of Chinese-Canadians as a whole. I wasn't proud of myself, but on the other hand, I still wanted to justify my reluctance, my ambiguity, and my lack of commitment. Being an opportunist is the cardinal sin of the first-generation immigrant, but anyone born and raised in Canada shouldn't use their lifelong status as a platform from which to look down on us.

My kids could grow up here, just like him.

The "final notice" was printed in red paper, the color of maple leaves in fall. The color of the country that was to become our new home. Suddenly the clouds in my mind began to separate and sun finally seeped through. I will return to Canada. I'll return for my children to grow up here, to live with integrity, free from schemes, calculations, and broken dreams.

In beautiful, beautiful, British Columbia, where for them the maple leaves turned red.

13

BECOME A BUTTERFLY AND FLY BY CHEONHAK KWON

TRANSLATED BY JOHN MOKRYNSKYJ AND HANA KIM

(for halmeoni)
Daughter!
Oh you daughter of man! Sister!
How cold and agonizing it must have been!
How lonely it must have been
to withstand that night
Of dark history that aches to the bone!
Although the sun has risen slowly,
It's still the break of dawn,
a morning with a corner darkened by shadow,

But spring has indeed come!
From between the railway ties over which cast iron wheels once ran,
A slender shoot soars up.
Oh look, there's a yellow dandelion flower
Blooming on its stem!

Wave your wings over the spring hillside where you once gathered greens,

The shepherd's purse flowers in the furrows of barley fields trembling in the breeze.
A little girl so chaste,The passing wind would bring a blush to her cheek.

Although you can't forget the torn skirt, The bruises on your chest,
Now open again the skirt you tidied with tears of blood And let the sunshine in.
Unlock the clot of blood with its warmth.
On this spring day
become a butterfly,
and fly up in glory.

Daughter!
Oh, daughter of Korea! Sister!

Author's Note:

This poem is for comfort women who were coerced into sexual slavery by the Imperial Japanese Army during World War II.

14

CROOKED TEETH BY DUNG KAI-CHEUNG

TRANSLATED BY NICK STEMBER

H met W at a speed dating event. It was the first time he'd tried that sort of thing. In the three years since his divorce, H hadn't made any friends of the opposite sex. After the normal 9 to 5, he watched sports or went out drinking with friends. Every other week his ex- wife would let him see their daughter, usually to go out to eat or see a movie. Time passed quickly and everything in his life was as orderly as in his work.

He was an orthodontist surgeon. As a dentist, he believed there wasn't a single thing in the world that couldn't be filled or set straight again. When his marriage started going sour, he treated it the way a dentist might treat a cavity. Sometimes it was poor hygiene, and sometimes people were just born that way. Whatever the case, cavities could be filled. In the worst cases, a root canal could be used, or braces to prevent future problems. If that didn't do the trick, the whole tooth could be pulled and replaced with an implant. The way technology was going, fake teeth looked just as good (and sometimes better) than real ones. For orthodontist surgeons like H, presentation was everything. It didn't matter if the teeth were real or not.

H didn't know why he'd gone to the speed dating event, but it wouldn't have been too far off to say that he was looking for a set of fake teeth. At his age, given the type of work he did and people he socialized with, it wasn't easy to meet that special someone. As a dentist, he wasn't opposed to the idea of seeking professional help.

He certainly wasn't about to waste his time baking butter cookies at a singles mixer, though, and the thought of going to 'afternoon tea' with hundreds of strangers terrified him. So in the end he'd settled on a romantic evening for six: three men and three women, they said, switching tables every twenty minutes. Just the level of commitment he was looking for.

H wasn't in a rush to find someone. He preferred to take things as they came. Arriving at the restaurant, he concluded that going on looks, he didn't have much of an advantage over the other two men. Even so, he felt confident.

The two older women weren't anything special, but they'd gone to some trouble with their makeup, so you could hardly say they were unattractive, either. In comparison though, the younger one was a breath of fresh air. In the first round, H was paired up with a middle-aged woman who claimed to be a lawyer. Perhaps trying to subvert stereotypes about emotionally cold lawyers, she did her best to catch his interest. But no matter how he tried, H couldn't stop his eyes from stealing away to the far end of the restaurant where they came to rest on the pretty young woman with long, black hair.

When it was finally H's turn, she introduced herself as W. Framed in shoulder-length hair, W's compact face seemed more delicate than it otherwise might. She was dressed plainly, in a long-sleeved shirt, with only her slender neck and hands exposed. H thought her pale skin made her look refined and frail, like a piece of china. If she had known a thing or two about makeup she might have even passed for beautiful. What a waste, H thought.

Worst of all though, even in the dim light of the restaurant, H's expertise told him that W had a serious problem with her teeth. It was obvious: the way she avoided moving her lips when she spoke; the way she covered her mouth when she ate, and from the way she did her best to smile with her mouth clamped shut. For most men, tricks like this would have probably been enough to hide the truth. But for someone who'd seen as many teeth as H, she was like a sinner trying to hide from the all-seeing eye of the Buddha himself. Even with her mouth shut, H could tell that her teeth were uneven. When a sudden sneeze caught W by surprise, despite her best efforts to turn away and use her napkin for cover, and despite the sneeze being exceptionally dainty and not at all inelegant, in that moment of grace, H's vision was like an x-ray, capturing a complete snapshot of W's oral situation. His ardor cooling, H made motions to leave. The already pitiful expression on W's face only grew more so.

After the speed dating event, H went on a second date with the lawyer. Nothing came of it. It was around this time H remembered poor W. It suddenly struck him that he could offer to help W by fixing her teeth. Although H wasn't the sort to go in for charity, his professional training compelled him to see a set of crooked teeth not only in terms of oral hygiene, but more fundamentally as a moral failure. Ugly teeth weren't just a private shame that kept a person from holding their head high — they were an offense to others. He'd spent his life crafting one perfect set of teeth after another, with the secret goal of giving every man, woman and child on earth the most perfect, beautiful smile. Many celebrities and people of note had been H's clients. Whenever he saw their faces on the news, he always felt a flush of pride, knowing that he'd made his own small contribution to the world. So when it came to W, it was perhaps not so accurate to say that he was concerned, as it was to say that he felt obliged to provide assistance. Or even, he thought, to right an injustice.

H set up his date with W at a steakhouse in a fancy hotel, knowing that it would be an awkward choice for W. When she arrived, innocent of H's schemes, he took note that she had taken more care with her makeup and clothing than she had at the speed dating event. Evidently, she expected something to come of the evening. H brushed his surprise aside, putting it down to his usual attention to detail. Since he was acting out of the goodness of his own heart, he didn't feel guilty for having led her on. In her skin-tight black dress, W was as stiff and clumsy as a patient who'd just been fitted with a new set of dentures. She shifted uncomfortably, like a snake trying to shed its skin. Biting into the bloody steak with her crooked teeth, she looked positively miserable, and even in the candlelight he could tell that her face had gone crimson. Catching her at her most defenseless, H launched his attack, saying: "You know, I'm a dentist."

Doing her best to chew, W swallowed the wad of meat in her mouth with some difficulty.

"Of course I know. That was one of things they mentioned at the dating service."

"Ah, but more specifically, I'm an orthodontist," H said.

W wasn't an idiot, so from her expression he could tell she understood his meaning immediately. Her eyes fluttered as she tried to hold back the tears now rolling down her face. Before H could comfort her, W said: "But that's the whole reason I went to that speed dating event! Thanks to my teeth, I've never been able to keep a boyfriend."

"Well, why not get them fixed? It's not that hard. It certainly isn't cheap, but not impossibly so. Besides, you're talking about something that makes such a big difference for dating..."

W shook her head.

"Why? Why would a person dislike me just because my teeth aren't straight? It just doesn't make sense!"

"You're not wrong. But think about it this way: shouldn't you be grateful that they're looking out for your best interests? If your boyfriend wants you to be more beautiful, and isn't too much trouble, then what's wrong with that?"

There was a long silence. Even though W wasn't stupid, you couldn't say she had a way with words, either. Going in for the kill, H adopted a joking tone, as if teasing a child. Smiling magnanimously, he said:

"Look, W, you're a very pretty girl. I'm serious! But you're letting your looks go to waste! Those teeth of yours are ruining everything. It's sad. If you're willing to let me help, I could — "

"Actually, you already did," W suddenly said, her slender neck like an eel shooting out of its hole to snatch up unsuspecting prey. Now it was H's turn to be speechless.

"I was a patient at your clinic fifteen years ago."

It was as an unexpected, as if he'd been punched in the mouth.

Flustered, H said:

"Is that so? Why didn't you — "

"I was too embarrassed. I recognized you right away. Do you

remember me now? I was nine years old, with an under-bite and teeth that went in, like this. So my mom took me to your clinic. You gave me a thick plastic retainer, like those mouth-guards that boxers wear. Then you had me wear headgear that covered my whole face. The top part rested on my forehead, and the bottom cupped around chin, with two little rubber bands that attached to the mouth-guard to pull my teeth forward, bit by bit. I felt like Frankenstein. I had to go around like that for six months until my teeth finally moved enough for me to chew again like a normal person.

"But there still wasn't enough space in my jaw, and the retainer had kept my adult teeth from coming in. Everything was so crowded there wasn't room for anything else. You told me that once all my teeth were grown in I'd have to get more treatment to straighten them out. Because of how bad it was, you were going to have to pull four teeth, and then give me braces. The whole process was probably going to take two or three years. You did impressions. I remember looking at the casts of my teeth pointing this way and that thinking that they looked like buildings after a landslide.

"But when it came time to pull those first four teeth I never showed up. I was so afraid that I spent the whole time crying in my room. Mom thought I just needed a good cry, and so she said we could go later. I never went through with it, though. It got more obvious as time passed, but I was really stubborn, you know? I thought, who says I have to have straight teeth? How come no one is going to like me just because I have crooked teeth? Isn't there anyone out there who doesn't care about my teeth? I decided I'd wait for my Mr. Right to show up."

As she talked, W writhed around in her dress even more than before. H realized that things were more complicated than he'd thought — W had deep rooted hang ups that were going to take time to resolve. H changed tack, trying to gain her trust, instead:

"And what if I said I think I'm that person?"

H's words caught W by surprise. She at stared him, trying to judge his sincerity.

"You should be the last person I'd fall for," she said finally. "But for some reason I can't stop thinking about you. Maybe it's because you understand teeth."

After the meal, H was surprised to find himself in the lobby with W, paying for a room in the hotel.

Arriving in the room, they tore off their clothing and began to explore each other's bodies like two half-starved beasts. Having finally shed her black snakeskin, W's soft white body was free to wrap itself around H in a boneless embrace. His perfectly tailored suit pooled like mud on the floor, they fell into a struggle between life and death in the primordial jungle.

At first, H self-consciously avoided W's mouth. After kissing every part of her, only the mouth remained as the last unknown, a virtual black hole. Having once dispassionately disposed of the catastrophe of her teeth, H reflected on how strange it was to find himself now recoiling from them in terror. Only, like a real black hole, the mouth seemed possessed of its own gravity, pulling him inexorably towards its center. *A necessary sacrifice,* he consoled himself. *He who'd have the tiger cub, must be a tiger club.*

Having braced himself for the final assault, H charged W's tiger's den, that yawning maw of teeth. W shrank back from him. But this only provoked his lust further. Sucking violently on her lips, he pushed his tongue deep into her mouth, like a greedy thief shoving his arm into a hidey hole, sweeping across the two rows of crooked teeth like a blind man reading braille, pressing on each and every tooth with the slender tip of his organ. H was shocked to find himself powerless to resist the pull of W's crooked teeth.

Their mouths fully interlocked, tongues ensnared, and teeth colliding like ping pong balls, he entered her, one organ mirroring another. Just when H thought he couldn't hold back the tide of pleasure any longer, W reached her own climax. Their mouths flew apart like a gas explosion and W sunk her crooked teeth deep into H's shoulder. He cried out in pain.

Exhausted, they lay panting on the hotel bed, while H held his hand over his shoulder. When he took it away he saw the palm was stained with blood. Twisting his neck, he tried to get a look at the wound, finally standing and walking over to the mirror. An irregular bite mark flashed on his right shoulder. When he pressed it with his finger he gasped from pain. In the mirror, W lay naked on the bed, as wide-eyed and innocent as a timber wolf. She called out to him, apologizing softly. Saying that she didn't mean it, she bit her lower lip with a protruding canine. H felt himself grow hot again, and so he turned and threw himself on her.

From that day on, the hotel became W and H's regular meeting place. After eating steak, they would go upstairs. H began demanding that W use her crooked teeth to bite him on different parts of his body. The shoulder, the arm, the chest, his stomach, the back, his ass, his thigh, his calf. His body was soon covered in bite marks. W didn't seem to mind. For her, it was just another sexual fetish. She only drew the line at touching his genitals with her mouth.

Although H tried to force her, every time she simply closed her mouth, refusing to budge. When H asked why, she said, "I'm afraid I'll hurt you." But he wondered maybe if W didn't trust him. And so it became the only taboo, an unfillable void.

On the days that H couldn't see W, the bite marks became precious souvenirs, like autographs proving W's existence and sustaining his lust. At home, he would strip naked and stand in front of the mirror, appreciating his battle scars the way some people admire tattoos. H caressed the raised scars on his skin, like a needle running through the grooves of a record, replaying every moaned curse of their sexual liaisons. He felt like he'd been transformed into a whole new person.

Back at the clinic, however, where everything was as bright and clean as it had always been, H found himself feeling out of place. The once shining devices and gleaming tools looked cold and unfeeling. His brain was filled with scenes of bloody, animal conquest. Faced with children and teens who came to have their teeth straightened, H found he had lost his former inspiration, dully and mechanically finishing his work without faith or enthusiasm.

Eventually he found himself developing a revulsion for straight teeth. His pretty little assistant, R, for example — when he'd hired her it was her perfect, pearly white teeth that had caught his attention. But now he felt nothing at all at the sight of her teeth. His rebukes became more pointed than before, and unlike in the past, her shining smile afforded no defense from his barbed criticisms.

After work, he caught sight of an enormous ad for the "Queen of Tutoring" cram school on the side of a bus. The teacher — his ex-wife

— was dressed in designer clothes like a celebrity, a wide smile revealing her absolutely flawless teeth. Those teeth had always been his pride and joy. When H had first given C braces, she was just a college student, majoring in English. Later, they'd fallen in love and gotten married. C was hired at a famous cram school, and between her looks and her ability to ace exams, she'd found quick success. Later, she started up her own cram school, the one that was in the ad. H had always felt he'd had something to do with her success. Even the divorce hadn't changed his conviction. Looking at his ex-wife now, though, lust was the furthest thing from his mind. He couldn't even appreciate her teeth anymore. If anything, they left him feeling wooden. All he could think about was W, counting the days until their next meeting.

Outside of her ferocity in the bedroom, H found W to be extremely mild-mannered. Whenever he needed her, she would be there for him, but she never complained if H was unable to see her. She said that she had always wanted to be a stewardess, but her teeth had kept her from getting past the application stage. Putting it this way was, of course, somewhat euphemistic, but he could guess what she meant. Since then, she'd worked a series of jobs where she didn't need to interact with customers, eventually taking an administrative position in the municipal government.

Whenever he thought about the ups and downs that W had suffered in life, H was sympathetic and sorrowful. This was true, even knowing that the source of W's shame was now his greatest point of attraction. The idea of making W his wife seemed somehow inappropriate, however. In the end, he decided they just needed more time.

That same morning, H's ex-wife had brought their daughter to the clinic for braces. C was, if nothing else, pragmatic, and even though they were divorced, they had stayed on good terms. Since her ex-husband was a famous orthodontist, after all, why not put him in charge of their daughter's big day? Besides, she'd always blamed H for passing down his genes for crooked teeth. And it was true, when he thought about it — his mother's teeth had looked like a chessboard at mid-game. He hadn't dealt with his own teeth until he decided to become a dentist. A dentist is the best advertisement for his own work after all.

Actually, his daughter's teeth weren't that bad. To listen to his wife talk, though, it was like she had a birth defect. Before, H would have probably agreed. As superfluous as it seemed to him now, he did as his wife asked, putting braces on their daughter. Halfway through, H blew up at his assistant again, yelling at her for the way she brought him his tools. R ran out of the room sobbing, and another hygienist came in to take her place. His ex-wife, meanwhile, who'd seen the whole thing, said he owed R an apology.

By lunch, H was in a foul mood. He was worried about W. They hadn't met in days now. She said she was busy, and wouldn't be able to see him until the weekend. When H rolled up his sleeves in the bathroom he noticed the bite mark from their last meeting had almost healed, leaving only a couple of disparate points. Placing the marks in his own mouth, he compared the shape of his mouth to W's. Driven to distraction, he called her. She wouldn't tell him where she was, but he was finally able to get her to agree to come and meet him.

To save time, H arranged to have W meet him in the room. After a half hour, the doorbell rang. H opened the door to a swollen and pale-looking W. Uncaring, H pulled her into the room, pinning her against the wall as he stripped her naked and tried to kiss her mouth. W unexpectedly turned her head away, struggling to hold him back. Lacking the strength to hold out against his attack, she finally went limp. H tasted blood, and thinking that he'd hurt her, paused. That was when he saw the blood on W's lips, her uneven gums looking like freshly chewed steak. She looked down and covered her mouth.

H said,"What's wrong? Why are you bleeding?"

"I had four teeth pulled this morning," W said, mumbling.

H didn't understand.

W looked up at him and tried to smile. "I decided to get braces."

"Why didn't you tell me?"

"Are you mad I didn't ask you to do it?" W's voice wavered.

"Of course not! That's not it at all!" H said, almost shouting.

"I wanted to surprise you!"

"You call that a surprise?"

"Aren't you happy I want to make my teeth more beautiful for you?"

"But how are you supposed to bite me with teeth like that?"

"I can still bite you with straight teeth! What difference does it make? If you want me to bite you, just say so!"

Because the anesthetic had numbed her lips, W was having trouble speaking clearly. Drool and blood pooled in the corners of her mouth. W didn't notice or didn't care, pressing on like a dying lover in a soap opera, offering up her final bite.

Merciless, H pushed W away, pulling his clothes back on as quickly as he could. Still not caring about appearances, W threw herself on H, but he shook her off easily, pulling open the door. Just before it closed, he shouted:

"Backstabber!"

Her reply came faintly through the door: "I did it for you! Everything was for you!"

Furious, H called the clinic to tell R to cancel all of his appointments for the afternoon. He followed his first impulse, walking in a nearby convenience store to buy a six-pack. Drinking as he walked, he set off in a random direction. Row after row of perfect teeth greeted him: healthy, straight, spotless, unblemished teeth, set in wide smiles, illuminated in blinding contrast in the window of every shop and every light box of every bus stop along the street. Seeing so many perfect teeth made him nauseous. Looking up at the sky, the buildings around him appeared crooked, and he felt dizzy, like he was going to pass out.

Falling to the ground, his mouth struck something hard, a bloody tooth falling out with the vomit.

It was late by the time H returned to the clinic but R still hadn't left. When R saw that he was drunk and bleeding from the mouth, she quickly got over her shock and fell into the nurturing role of her profession. Bringing H to one of the chairs, she gently cleaned his gums and the cut on his lip. For R, it was a dream come true, but H was oblivious. Grabbing her suddenly, he ignored the piercing pain in his mouth, kissing R on the mouth.

After a moment's struggle, R gave in, the two of them embracing awkwardly under the fluorescent lights of the operating room. After a moment of fondling, their clothes only half removed, H frantically tried to enter her. But when he saw R's perfectly white teeth in her open mouth, arranged like two rows of soldiers in a ceremonial parade, H felt himself go flaccid. Disappointed, R pretended like nothing was the matter, tidying up her uniform. It was clear that his sudden disinterest hurt even worse than being yelled at.

H soon found himself alone in the clinic. His phone buzzed, a text message from W:

"I only did it for you, but then I found out that you're not the one I'd been waiting for. You don't love me after all. We're done."

Full of remorse, H felt an aching pain deep in his chest. When he tried to type a reply, he found he had nothing to say. He set the phone down and placed a finger in his mouth, feeling for the gap where his tooth had been. The painful, empty feeling reminded him of something. He walked over to the storage room, and unlocked the door.

Going through the cabinets one by one, in an out of the way corner of the room, he finally found what he was looking for. Usually he would give away the plaster impressions as a gift to celebrate a patient's last appointment, or throw them away if the patient didn't want theirs.

Since W had never come back, he had kept her impressions. Most amazing of all, though, was the fact that the unclaimed mold had survived a move to a new clinic several years back.

But there was W's name, clearly written on the tag. Taking the impressions back with him to the operating room, he tore open the plastic bag and carefully placed the contents on the table.

The two halves of W's jaw lay on the table like seeds scattered at random. The crooked teeth were as familiar as a dead loved one. Rubbing them with one finger, he felt a shiver of electricity run down his spine. It was as if the false teeth had become real.

He took off his shirt and picked up the upper jaw mold, pressing it as hard as he could into his left bicep, leaving a semi-circle of crooked teeth imprinted in his flesh. He repeated the process, biting his own shoulder, his own chest, his own stomach. Finally, he put the impressions back on the table and pulled down his pants, unable to restrain himself any longer.

H cried out in pain.

Amid the jagged forest of snow-white teeth, moist beads of spring dew flowed, the translucent fluid threaded with the merciless, red blood of a bird devoured.

15

9 MEDITATIONS ON POETRY & MANDOPOP BY JASMINE GUI

The first metaphor I understood intuitively is the moon as a heart — an image floating off the ubiquitous vocals of Teresa Teng's 月亮代表我的心. It is a song that has captivated the Chinese-speaking community for decades, a Chinese metaphor no one else will ever claim, yet also an image that compels hundreds of artists to re-appropriate, manipulate, and refashion it. It is a Chinese moon to Shakespeare's rose.

A good metaphor is a ripple from the centre of a voice to the world.

Hebe 田馥甄 released 渺小 in 2013, a song based on Wislawa Symborzka's "Under One Small Star". Her lyrical performance leaves me as awestruck as the English translation of the poem does with its quiet, powerful tone. I often try to imagine the beauty I cannot understand in the Polish original, and all the other languages it now exists in. I marvel at how emotions can cross so many thresholds to speak in some way to a listener. I realize how many thresholds a single listener might have.

. . .

How should I write poetry that crosses these thresholds?

When thinking up names for our literary magazine, the word "LooseLeaf" surfaces, after 野子 by Sue 蘇運瑩. The sound of "the wild" (yé zi), so similar to the Chinese sound for "leaves" (yè zi), compels me, as well as her dense, tumbling lyrics and unique voice. I think about what it means to put a magazine together for young Asian artists in Canada, and wish that same wild ambition and courage of the song fills the pages of every copy we print and put out into the world.

I realize LooseLeaf is a one-word poem that you could call a prayer.

The first song I pick at karaoke is A-Sang 阿桑's 葉子. I know and love it well but I am too anxious, and cannot finish the song for all the blood pounding in my head. I am afraid to be heard and evaluated by those listening. I am afraid because I am unfamiliar with the sound of my voice. I come back to this experience often, whenever I am frustrated with my words.

After all, being a writer is about trying to finish the song.

I sit at a cafe with Vincent Fang 方文山's 青花瓷 and try to decipher the classical Chinese grammar and sentence structures he employs with so much ease. I mark up the lyrics the same way I would with the poetry I study, trying to learn the logic of its rules.

. . .

The afternoon shows me how syntax is the spine and ribcage of a piece of writing. It protects the heart of the poem.

If I could spend a day with an artist, I would pick vocalist and lyricist A-shin 阿信 from 五月天. The 6-minute long 如煙 from Mayday's seventh album is a song with no repeating lines. The song is an example of how you might say one thing in so many ways. I think you can only do this by paying close attention to this world and to the things in it. I would ask A-shin over tea what kind of world he sees. I am curious.

Poetry is seeing and hearing with my own senses, and speaking in my own voice.

A writer has a voice that takes on appearances, cadences and tones. Ayal Komad 張震嶽 teaches me this. 愛我別走 and 自由 are enduring classics from his 1998 album that showcases the versatility of his voice as a rapper and a singer. More interestingly, his 2014 album is weighted with the last 16 years of growth. When I listen to it, I hear an artist leaving things behind and following his voice. I am reminded that words and works should not box me in.

As an artist I also grow out of words like old skin.

These days I begin to come into the presence of music aging. Some remnant of me occasionally recognizes the ballad tunes and mellow vocals from the early movies and restaurant radios of my childhood. When I listen to Karen Mok 莫文蔚's 愛情, I think that what is present enough will trickle through time, washing their own paths into different histories.

I feel a strong desire for my words to make their way through days and years into another person's life.

Poetry is a homecoming. It says what you cannot say but always know. Poetry is about recognition. Cozy Diary 輕日記's 一個人曖昧sounds like recognition expanding in me on a solitary afternoon. I would like to be a writer people look for on the days they want company, to share the silence of that moment, fill the emptiness of that day, or remind them of something they might be in the middle of forgetting.

I would like people to make their homes in my poems.

Author's Note:

This is a love letter to the music that has traveled with me throughout my life. The genesis of my poetry writing begins with Mandopop: lyric scraps spinning in my head like the discman I carried everywhere in the early 2000s. My poetry often chases after and yearns to emulate the embodied experience of listening to Chinese music. As I keep negotiating what it means to be a bilingual writer who draws so much from one language to write mostly in another, Chinese music continues to show me how it is possible to feel in language, regardless of what that language is, and how the most important thing is to always be listening.

SONGS

The Moon Represents My Heart by Teresa Teng Insignificance by Hebe Tien

Wild Thing by Su Yunying Leaves by A Sang

Blue and White Porcelain by Jay Chou, written by Vincent Fang As Smoke by Mayday

Love Me, Don't Go and Free by Chang Chen-Yue/Ayal Komad Love by Karen Mok

Uncertain with Myself by Cozy Diary

16

ON LOSS BY JOANNE LEOW

When they tell me that my mother can no longer write
I like to think of it as a loss of fine motor control
I don't like to remember the cards she once
sent me, her sharp angular writing,
the messages getting imperceptibly terser
over the years, what may have been the last card or note
Misplaced in a shoebox or folder,
Or what her handwriting might look like now
They say this atrophy could be reversed
if there was inspiration or inclination.
But I don't believe that, I prefer not
to think about my mother's
failing hands, fingers, or will at all
as if dwelling on them too much would be
a premonition of sorts
I prefer to think of the
box that one ticked for a toddler's developmental
goals, a skill improved by tiny pieces of plastic
that fit into each other, by tying endless bits of
string into knots and then unknotting them again.

I like to think of the carefully cut and glued stars on preschool projects,
of folding minuscule cranes from washi paper.

But that is simply a ruse:
while we briefly rise above
our bodies and time, to live
is to lose
everything.

17

PRE-ELEMENTARY, MY DEAR MONKEY BY LINDA NGUYEN

Dad drove me across the Lachapelle Bridge in his red '85 Pontiac and I could see the sun rising above the river. I wasn't old enough to sit in the front yet. I only turned five last winter. Geese overhead in a V-shape formation speared through the sky, chanting honks on the way. The orange rays from the orb hanging above the water filtered through the spaces and cracks between the vertical beams of the steel bridge, and into Dad's car. As he drove, staccatos of warm light flashed across the headrest in front of me. The same happened on the pleated plaid skirt of the black and forest-green overalls I wore to school.

The bridge connected two islands: my new suburban home in the city of Laval, where my parents and I moved last summer, and my private preschool in Montréal.

It was spring. I couldn't recite the months in English by heart yet, but I knew it was March, as in, I knew it in Vietnamese. The leaves on the resilient trees on each side of the river were sprouting. It was the landscape of an incongruent haircut with a shimmery bald spot where the river flowed, parts of it still frozen, separating the two masses of trees. Dad didn't have a bald spot though. He had a full head of black hair, and Mom plucked away his white hairs now and then because he didn't like them. Mom could find anywhere between ten to forty of them each time. I sat in the backseat to the right of my dad. Not a single white hair in sight.

Once we were off the bridge, Dad turned right at the second set of lights, passed the ice-cream shop that was now closed. It had a dingy sign of a soft serve ice-cream cone hanging above the window. Next to it was a karate school.

"Before I woke you up this morning," Dad said, "I saw you waving your arms and punching the air."

"... No I wasn't."

"Sure you were. Who were you punching? Ghosts?"

"I don't remember."

"I want you to start karate lessons. Good for health and for self-defence."

"But what if I don't like it?"

"I'll start karate too."

"Okay," I said, persuaded by the mere idea that Dad would be there with me, doing karate, but he didn't tell me that children and adults didn't train together.

"If anyone bullies you at school, you'll be able to defend yourself," he said. "No one is allowed to hurt my daughter."

"Like this?" I threw punches in the air, but my arms were too short to even graze the seat in front of me. Dad smiled. He stopped at a red light.

"You'll have a full schedule along with your swimming lessons, Vietnamese lessons, and your new piano lessons. It's good. You'll be prepared for anything."

"Okay," I said. I didn't want to disappoint him.

The light turned green. He drove up and parked his car behind a small yellow bus and walked me across the school lawn towards the entrance reserved for preschool children. He never wanted me to hop out of the car and run in like all the other kids. Dad wanted to make sure I made it in safely and in a dignified manner. My French teacher, the tall and slender Mme Claire, held the door open with her foot. I had never seen her copper-brown hair in anything but a ponytail.

"Bonjour Amy," she said. "Good morning Mr. Tran."

"Good morning."Dad nodded. When he smiled, his temples puffed up above and under the metal arms of his wire framed glasses, creasing them.

He crouched down to meet me at eye level, turned his clean-shaven face to the side and said "Give me a kiss," in our language. Once I did, he kissed me back on the forehead on my hairline, the kind of Vietnamese kiss where he'd suck in air through his nose while holding my head in his firm, protective hands.

I said "bye-bye" to him and I grinned with my tongue pressed through the hole of my first missing front tooth, the one I lost from biting into a cookie during Snack Time the other day, but Mme Claire put my tooth in a Ziploc bag and said it was okay. I sauntered through the doors of École Bellechasse, down the hall, and into my bilingual class, but the least bilingual child was me. My English was passable, but the French language was still foreign and alien to me. My brain had to work harder. Sometimes, it was like learning to tie my shoelaces, but the French words kept getting tangled around my fingers. I knew a handful of words; I just couldn't tie them together into coherent sentences.

In the classroom, no one was playing with the Tangram, my new favourite puzzle, a set of blocks with different colours and shapes. It came with a set of cards, each with a silhouette of an animal or thing. Yesterday, I made a cat. The day before that, a swan. I needed to hurry in order to get to it before anyone else. I skedaddled over to my coat hook, the one with my laminated name on pink construction paper taped over it. My spring coat slid off my shoulders, and I shoved my red Rubbermaid lunch box under the bench. Off I went.

"Don't run, Amy!" my English teacher Ms. Sara said. Her gaze followed me, but not a single blond spike from her short pixie haircut moved. Once I got to the Tangram, it was too late. A boy named Lucas got there first.

"After, it's my turn," I declared, but he paid no attention. He was too absorbed in building his sailboat. He didn't finish building the hull yet when he destroyed the mainsail to build something else, disregarding the cards with the silhouettes on them. My turn wasn't going to come unless I tattle-taled, a word often thrown around in the classroom.

The rest of the class had already stormed in. Ms. Sara took

attendance, her blue earring clusters swishing back and forth as she wrote a checkmark beside a name.

"Erika Tomlin? She's here... Amy Tran? "She said over a rambunctious sea of forest-green polo sweaters and dark slacks, white blouses and dress overalls.

"Present," I said. I was only a round table away. All the tables were set up around the classroom with four or five chairs at each one. At the center was cleared floor space the size of two living rooms, maybe three, delineated by red tape to form a rectangle.

I gave up the Tangram and played a half-hearted game of stacking wooden cubes in order of size on a square carpet under the classroom windows. All the cubes were of a faded thulian pink, chipped at the corners.

On my first day of school, this was the first toy I encountered. When Mme Claire showed it to me, I often pointed to other toys that kept the other thirty-some children delighted and busy, but I couldn't speak a word of English or French to tell her I wanted to try those other games. Her constant refusal and my inability to argue constrained me to this single set of blocks. I was taller than half my classmates, the top of my head reaching Mme Claire's waist, but I felt little and silenced. Not only that, but I had to stack them by size. It was the only correct way to play. I couldn't tell her I already understood the concept of big and small. I also couldn't tell her I knew I was the only kid who wasn't allowed to play with the other toys, as if being unable to speak English or French made me too stupid to play with them.

My intelligence was judged proportionate to how many western words I knew, and that was a repertoire of zero. I kept talking in Vietnamese, expecting Mme Claire to understand, but she hadn't a clue. I could only speak to her with my hands. Two classmates walked by. They said something to each other and then laughed. Mme Claire frowned at them and they left.

A few days later, I learned how to say "It's not fair."

I went home and repeated those words whenever rules applied to me and no one else.

I had to be in bed by what my parents called "9 pm" while they were still awake to watch a movie. "It's not fair."

I had to have my ears pierced at the mall when I didn't want to. It hurt too much. Dad didn't have his ears pierced. "It's not fair."

I had to eat everything on my plate every dinner or I couldn't leave the table, whereas the food that my mom or dad couldn't finish, Mom stored them in containers and placed them in the fridge, calling them "leftovers." "It's not fair."

I kept saying those words, often with my arms crossed and sometimes while in tears, until Mom's capacity to endure me was breached. She raised her palm.

"*Con không được nói 'not fair' nữa. Nói nữa là mẹ đánh đòn.*" You're not allowed to say "not fair" anymore, she said. Any more and I'll spank you.

So I stopped.

I had been at École Bellechasse for seven months. It was now March. I could speak to both my teachers, but not as well as the other children. I was allowed to play with half the toys in the classroom, including the Tangram, but not the other half. I mixed up June and July when I recited the months, but I could count to ten in three languages. I learned from English and French that blue and green were separate colours, while in Vietnamese, they were one and the same. Màu xanh meant both, unless I specified it as the green of the leaves on trees, or the blue of the sky.

I abandoned my pink wooden cubes and looked out the window. More geese flew through the blue, and disappeared in the distance behind buildings and trees. I didn't know they were geese yet. I just called them the birds who were coming back from their vacation.

The end of the school day came and all the kids were ushered to the hanging coats lining the wall next to the classroom entrance. Once we were all dressed to go outdoors and armed with our backpacks and lunchboxes, we hurried to the center of the class, forming two lines in order to exit the classroom in a disciplined fashion. There was an odd number of us kids, so whoever wasn't fast enough had to stand alone at the back. I didn't want that.

Ms. Sara stood at the front. She raised an index finger to her lips.

"Okay, no more talking." Her earring clusters froze in place, but we were still discharging energy with our yapping mouths and our restless arms and legs. "I'm going to count to three," and that scared us each time. "One, two... two and a half —" but some of us still dared to whisper "— and three."

Dead silence. And then a whimper.

"On ne parle plus," Mme Claire said from the back of the line.

"No more talking," Ms. Sara repeated.

I started to hum. I had a song in my head. It wasn't talking. I knew the difference.

"Whoever talks will be the little monkey at the back," she said.

No fear. I wouldn't be the little monkey because I wasn't talking. I believed no one could hear me. Only I could hear myself hum. No one had to listen.

"Who's talking?" Ms. Sara said. She walked up the two lines and lingered midway through, sticking her ear out, the blue cluster hanging from her earlobe swaying back and forth."I said no talking." She leaned in towards me. "Amy, you're talking."

"No, I'm not."

"To the end of the line."

She looked angry and she made me walk to the back where Mme Claire stood. My classmates started their chatter.

"Didn't I say no talking?" Ms. Sara said, but no one listened because she wasn't counting down to three.

I wondered why I had to be standing alone when there could be a line of three at the back. I could merge with the two girls in front of me. I tried to wiggle my way in between them, but Mme Claire held my shoulders, keeping my feet planted in front of hers. My English teacher stood at the front again.

"Amy was talking. Now, she's the little monkey," she said.

Thirty-some heads turned to look at me and laughed. I started to cry.

"Let's try again. No more talking," Ms. Sara said. She started the countdown, but I couldn't stop the tears from streaming, nor the strange sounds in my mouth from surfacing.

"Ne pleure pas Amy," Mme Claire said.

"No crying," said Ms. Sara, but I couldn't stop.

Why didn't she specify that humming wasn't allowed? Why were my teachers specific about not crying when I couldn't stop?

In front of me, one girl whispered into the ear of the other girl.

The latter giggled.

So I punched her.

"Amy! Non!" Mme Claire said.

"That's it," said Ms. Sara, "you're sitting on the red line. Amy will be the last to leave."

No! Not the red line! It was worse than being the little monkey. It meant sitting to the side and being looked down upon as they left.

The others chuckled among themselves. The two rows before me left through the doors at the sound of the school bell. I sat crossed- legged on the red tape that made a rectangle around the classroom, the windows and the pink wooden cubes at my back. I had my face in my hands. I didn't move from my spot for what felt like a long time, my bottom glued to the red line. Mme Claire made me blow my nose in a tissue. When I looked up, Dad was at the door with his usual work cap on his head and his employee badge around his neck. It dangled in front of his white dress shirt that was striped in thin lines of grey. He was talking to Ms. Sara. I got up and ran to him. He picked me up and I wound my arms around his neck.

"Don't forget your lunchbox," Ms. Sara said. She handed it to my dad, but I couldn't care about it. I hated her.

Dad pushed out the school doors and stepped outside, on to the lawn. All the other kids were gone.

"Ah, my little monkey," he said. He kissed my damp cheek, sucking air in through his nose the way he did this morning.

"I'm not a monkey!"

"Okay, okay. You're not a monkey." He kissed me again. "*Giỏi, ba thương.*" Be good and I'll love you, I heard him say, but I didn't know how to be good.

We got to my dad's red car and I climbed into the backseat. I wiped my eyes and he gave me my lunchbox. He drove across the bridge. We were heading home.

The bridge didn't just connect two islands; it connected two distinct but similar worlds: one governed by parents, the other run by teachers.

"It's not fair," I said.

"What's not fair?"

"Everything."

18

WHAT I LEARNED FROM MY PIANO LESSONS BY LI CHARMAINE ANNE

You've never played pentatonic scales on a guqin or pipa, but you do have a diploma in piano. On cool summer nights, you even make it a habit to strum a guitar at campfires. Western music, you believe, is a book you've read in depth enough to declare yourself an expert. It is a book of many chapters, but if you were asked, the building blocks of music are surely harmony, rhythm, and melody.

Harmony is the CDs you listen to in the family sedan, in the back seat during weekend grocery runs to Richmond. Dad air-conducts. Mom turns the volume knobs right and left as required. The car plays mostly Mozart and Tchaikovsky, with some Bach, Vivaldi and Chopin sprinkled in. Like leaning your head into the bend of the seatbelt, Mozart's "Piano Concerto No. 21" cradles you to sleep as you cruise over the Fraser River, and Tchaikovsky's "1812 Overture" makes you dance out of the doors, up and at attention. That Overture is a love affair you share with your father: you both understand how the first two minutes of layered cello, wrapped in a thick harmonic fabric, are the best two minutes. Your father shows you photos of himself with his university operetta cast — there's him, crouching in the front of the cast with a proud smile. Your mother is elsewhere in the chorus. Somehow, whatever harmonized their relationship — mutual fatigue at late night rehearsals? Witty conversations slipped between ticket- selling afternoons? — made you. It's funny, your audio preferences as an adult are so disparate from theirs, like when you pretend pretension by hanging around uptown theatres moshing to obscure local bands. You still hear your mother hum the harmonies of folk songs when you walk past the bathroom sometimes, a taste of nostalgia hiding in her throat. At midnight, your father taps on your door and complains that the cacophony of synth pads, guitar riffs, and bass lines growling and grinding in your room is too raucous for a neighbourhood of retirees.

Rhythm is discipline, the discipline it takes to learn to twist and leap and roll your fingers across eighty-eight black and white rectangular buttons. Rhythm keeps you home and makes you turn down play-dates as a tween, and it is a rhythm of habit that keeps you sane by dividing hours-long practice sessions into smaller increments. You vary from playing a measure over and over, to anger-releasing push-up breaks, to energy-replenishing-chocolate-bar-breaks, to I-want-to-lie-down- and-kill-myself breaks. All for the especial privilege of thundering out Chopin's "Fantasie-Impromptu" in any room with a piano and impressing all within listening vicinity — mostly adults. Any kid present twists uncomfortably in their chair knowing their mother will compare them to you. Because, while other children curse their parents' souls and quit, you chose this path for yourself. Unlike them, you appreciate the fatigue, the muscle cramps, the hours lost. Your father says that once you conquer this black-and-white behemoth of an instrument you can conquer anything, and you believe him to your bones. Your final exam is hard, but the exams and contests before that, including paper exams on harmony, counterpoint, history, and analysis, are harder. You receive your piano diploma before receiving your high school diploma, and perhaps piano helps you get into university.

But then you become old enough to dare ask: "Is this an Asian thing?" Because really, you're just one musical instrument-playing, acne-ridden, spectacle-wearing Asian immigrant child out of thousands. Thousands who become better than you, like the boy you grew up with down the street. He's playing with the national orchestra while you play within your four white walls. And what about all those kids in Europe, what do they do? All the world's symphonies and concertos, operas and musicals, come from that continent, yet all you ever seem to see are prodigies with straight black hair, Anglicized surnames, and an ambitious mother never too far away. Maybe you'll go to France one day, to the hometowns of composers like Ravel and Debussy, Fauré and Satie, artists you learn to admire after all exams and the contests and the hours spent perfecting "Fantasie Impromptu" were over. So, as you mark theory homework for neighbourhood kids, you wonder why it's such an overdone trope for East Asian parents to make their kids learn violin and piano. Is it a brand of internalized racism, of longing for the "civilized west"? Or is it for training of the mind, to "conquer anything," as your father still says? White people have hockey and basketball, after all, so maybe that leaves Asian people with piano and violin.

You think back to all the kids who played instruments with a feverish ambition when you were growing up. Well, most of that feverish ambition was not theirs but their parents'. Sometimes, when a song isn't working out, you wonder how much of your passion is yours. You've cursed music before, when your arms had streaks of pain shooting through the bone, when you knew, looking at prodigies on the internet, that you really weren't that good anyway. But the pain became a part of your skeleton, and you barely remember not knowing how to read music, the same way you barely remember not knowing how to read. When the diploma and frame arrive in a package outside, your parents proudly hammer it to the wall above the piano in the living room. It still hangs alone on the white wall, but you don't look that far up whenever you pass by.

Two words knock around in your head: for what?

Maybe you did it to impress adults and to make the family proud. To have a back-up career. Or because you started, went past the point of no return, and had to get it over with anyway.

You close the piano lid. When the exams for the neighbourhood kids are over, you don't mark the homework for their next one. Even though you'd be paid as someone with a diploma, you'd rather they bump each other on scooters than do homework that isn't even for school.

But music lingers. After all, melody is desire. It is pursuing and longing for something pure and true and meaningful that you want but can't name. You ponder and paw for melody especially now in your twenties, when words like "degree" and "career" penetrate your inbox. This is why the piano stands regal in the living room with a dusty veneer while the guitars and recording software in your room, earned through a string of part-time jobs, are polished and new. In the evenings after an eight-hour workday, when you collapse your bones upon a chair, you begin your search for melody. You pick up a guitar and sing without shame, trying the taste of notes and syllables, pausing to lean over and pen down a couplet with questionable rhyme. You curse your incompetent short-term memory as you struggle to record and write and hold on to a brilliant tune before your distracted mind loses it. What you want most is melody. Words and harmonies are ornamental to you, but melody is your star actress, the beautiful lead that vibrates the insides of your audience in a dazzling performance. After all, through all the musical phases of your teens, Mozart, the king of melody, remains the only human who can make your body shake. When the "Gran Partita" begins, a lone oboe pierces through a lull of gentle brass, halting spacetime with its voice. Halting your thoughts.

Is this what drugs feel like? You close your eyes and music becomes a lucid dream. It crosses the border from the theoretical to the physical; it becomes audial and visual. Pumping rhythms are stories of skyscrapers that build themselves up and up and around you into the sky. Cityscapes pulse and vibrate as they transform in and out of differing shapes and patterns. And you're flying, flying through a surreal world that you and sound continuously create deep in the crevasses of your mind.

So you look at the eighty-eight keys in your living room and ask a question you've asked yourself since you were a kid learning "Mary had a Little Lamb." Will you ever find the one melody that is yours, one that explains?

Your colleagues have all gone home. You shut down the computers, tidy up the counters, turn key in lock. You walk down silent, dim hallways where the humming of background machinery is the only music. You jump on a bus and sit down, watching the trees go by at the same rhythm as the music in your headphones. You come home and toss your keys into a basket. Drop your heavy knapsack upon the floor. You stretch your arms and wander into the dining room. The house is empty. The house is yours.

It's a fair day. You twist open the blinds and the last streams of sunlight filter through. Commuters have left the main road nearby, so the silence lets birdsong in. You lift the lid off your piano, sweep off the burgundy felt covering, and sit down at the bench. You lay your fingers on the keyboard, gently, almost with a flourish; it's muscle-memory from all those competition days, so who can blame you, flourishing within your private home? One breath — and then you begin — the first two pensive notes of Debussy's "Claire de Lune."

Your piano teacher once mentioned that she didn't allow too many students to attempt this piece because it was not easy, both technically and emotionally. You've always been a little smug about this. But that was years ago, and this is now. You guide your fingers through the one piece you have practiced the longest and abandoned the latest, and despite a few initial hiccups, its melody has never left your tendons as your fingers craft out the notes. They know how to put slightly more pressure on the fingers that outline the melody. They know how to tumble like gymnasts across the keys in the middle un poco mosso section. And in the theme's last re-statement, you meet your favourite part: an intentional, extra C-flat in the theme that discerns it from the introduction. You find this one note — able to convey just the right amount of nostalgic finality — a true stroke of genius.

For once, you stop obsessing over your life and think of Debussy instead. Not as a French composer, but as a man gazing alone at the moon with manuscript paper open on his lap. Just like that Chinese poem your parents quote now and then, that one by Li Bai:

Moonlight shines before the bed:
Can it be frost upon the ground?
I lift my head and see the moon —

Lower it, and think of my hometown.

Author's note:

This is an original translation created after reading many attempted English translations shared on the web and doing a fair bit of Google-Translating. The original Chinese: 床前明月光/ 疑是地上霜/ 舉頭望明月/ 低頭思故鄉.

19

A CURVE IN CONSTELLATION BY STANFORD CHEUNG

I share a wolf howl
head pointed
all afternoon
of fragmented
doings
left/ right
in a pack
pre urges
worn over
dawn
in the sky
like the fingers of Cancer
with an
intervened
Y
staring into itself
for a moment in space
The white sea.
a half-moon
swimming inside

for days
for weeks
by possibilities
awake
a riot
calm
an income field
eyeing the wind
eyeing the rain
giving in
mute fashions
firsthand
with every flower
of a
face scraped mosaic
an afterthought lesion
topless in the sentence
somehow calloused
a gathered poise
as inwardly
from reality
stippled presences
ignited remains
without
some compass of fate
paged pages
unforeseen ashes
nameless shapes
twisted gold
of a spirit
like esprit
falling apart
to ascertain standing
making certain that silence
a nursery rhyme
to my questions

on found
stressed leaves
seeking singularity
like a field
onto childhood
this sentence

20

ARTEFACTS, TWO WAYS BY RAINE LING

I was nine years old and doing my business in the bathroom, wholly absorbed in the Archie comic on my lap, when I was interrupted by a quiet cry coming from down the hallway. After flushing and washing my hands, I peeked through the crack in the bathroom door to investigate. It was my dad, sobbing in front of the washing machine in our basement. He had not heard the flush, and did not know I could see him. I didn't dare declare my presence; even at nine, I understood that this vulnerability was not something he would want me to see.

This crying was a private act — one I knew my naive, childish eyes should not be witnessing. But I continued to watch through the crack of the door. I watched my dad pick up each piece of clothing from the hamper, examining the garment slowly, wistfully, before dropping it into the machine. I watched for at least 45 minutes, wondering how many sweaters, t-shirts, pajamas, and adult undergarments he would need to get through before reaching the bottom of the hamper.

He hadn't cried at the funeral. I remember being angry. This was a simple emotion, one that surely a grown man could feel, if I could. *Aren't you sad?* I screamed, through tears, kicking his shins. But he stayed expressionless and simply hugged me, and we sat together for the rest of the afternoon in our own silence — save for the dissonant, repetitive chants coming from the traditional Cantonese singers that my *poh poh* and *gong gong* hired for the ceremony. I remember fiddling with the edges of my scratchy black dress while my dad followed along in the songbook they provided us. His index finger traced each line of the song. *Don't you wish you could read Chinese so you could follow along too, Lucy?* he asked me in Cantonese. *This is why you should pay more attention in Chinese school,* he said with a shake of his head, in a tone that suggested I should be ashamed of myself.

But now, believing he was alone, in our basement, he was crying. His crying was neither loud nor dramatic, and had I not heard the first soft cry, I might not have known he was crying at all. He picked up a white blouse — one that she had worn for his birthday a few weeks ago. He held it in front of his face, said something barely audible from the bathroom I was still hiding in. Was it *I miss you?* Or perhaps he was simply reading the washing instructions aloud, so as to not damage the silk. I knew it was from the birthday celebration because of the chocolate stain on the sleeve. I knew it because I remembered laughing at the ice cream explosion, stupidly, naively, ignorant of our impending misfortune. After a brief moment, he removed the blouse from his face, and it, too, was dropped into the machine, another artefact from what would now be my old life, diluted, washed away.

I later found out that the white blouse and the rest of the garments were going to be donated. I was supposed to come with him to help load and unload the bags of clothing at the Salvation Army. I refused, bursting into tears, insisting that we keep them all. My father just furrowed his brow, looking disappointed. His face pleaded, somewhat hopelessly, for me to stop my fit. *Lucy — now it has become too bitter of a past. We try not to hold onto the bitterness, okay? It hurt. So we donate the clothing. And you help me unload bags from car.* He spoke firmly, and in English, which told me he was more upset than usual. But I felt no sympathy. I wanted to hit him.

I did the verbal equivalent. *Oh ho zung lai ah!* I really hate you, I told him, a phrase I had only ever heard on Cantonese soap operas. And then in English, *You don't even miss her*, fully aware of my words: cold, cutting, drawn out — the image of him in front of the laundry machine holding the white blouse, vivid as ever.

After that trip to the Salvation Army, I quickly learned that my father had decided to keep nothing of hers in their old shared closet. Half the space was simply empty now. But his side of the closet remained intact, carefully arranged. He never spread his own shirts and ties out, never made full use of the space. I knew because for weeks after the funeral, I would creep into his room after he fell asleep, look inside shelves, investigate the corners of the room, peek behind the curtains, scavenging for remnants of my old life that I could add to my collection. Within a few weeks of this habit, I amassed a wide variety of artefacts: my mom's old paper planner, a chequebook, and her favourite hat, which he had accidentally forgotten to include in the donation pile.

In the darkness, I could often make out the faint outline of my dad sleeping, on his usual side of the bed (the left). I noticed that he never bothered to shift to the middle. The middle was where I had sometimes slept whenever my childhood insomnia struck me, able to rest only after being sandwiched between the warmth of my parents' bodies, only after clenching my already asleep mother's hand, only after feeling this small comfort — one that told me she was there, even if not awake.

These days, about once a month, I return to a home that looks almost identical to the one I knew in my childhood. There's a few old family portraits, including my parents' wedding photo in the living room, a decade-old, hand-drawn father's day card and a bunch of fake crystal swans lining our fireplace mantle, plastic wrap on some of our furniture and looped around our TV remote. There are small changes of course, ones that are subtle and to be expected after the course of seventeen years. There's a flat screen plasma TV where the boxy, black one used to be. My dad wears slippers around the house now. There are Chinese tabloids, ones that he gets from the grocery store a few kilometers away, strewn across the couches. It's a little less tidy than I remember it being in my childhood, but then again, why bother being neat when you're the only one to see the mess?

Tonight, I can tell that my dad is happy to see me. He's always content with my visits, but this time it's a little more: he greets me with a smile and a pat on my shoulder. I take off my shoes and enter the kitchen, and a mixture of savoury aromas fills the air around me. I feel myself salivating — my dad's cooking has always been my favourite. I smell pork congee with bits of preserved, salted and century eggs sprinkled throughout, and a platter of thick, chewy udon noodles with slices of steak, red peppers, onions and mushrooms.

My dad opens the fridge, cracks open a bottle of Tsingtao beer. He doesn't bother to offer me one; his daughter doesn't drink beer, of course. She is good, everything he wanted her to be, for the most part. I don't bother to tell him about the hangover I have, or the stranger who woke up in my bed this morning. We talk on the phone every other day, but we are worlds apart. We know everything and we know nothing of each other, all at once. We are family, and we are strangers.

He ladles congee into two bowls, passing them to me to set on the placemats. I'm reminded of Sunday morning lunches from years ago, the three of us forming a right angle triangle sitting around the table, my mother beside my father, my father across from me, my parents talking business about the shop, while I sat in silence; mute, unheard, aside from the occasional slurp of congee entering my mouth.

Habit's a funny thing. We sit down, in the arrangement we've sat in our whole lives, though now we form a line instead of a triangle. I'm starving, and immediately pour the congee into my mouth in huge spoonfuls, occasionally interrupting this motion with a bite of noodle. *Ho ho mai ah!* Really tasty, I tell him with childish earnestness, my mouth full. I look up from my bowl and see him chuckling at my gluttony, my lack of manners. He's smiling, but he looks tired. His head is entirely grey these days. The textures on his face, the craters for eye bags — they look like they belong to a man in a nursing home, not someone in their late fifties. I can tell he's lost weight recently; his polo shirt hangs off his body, looking one size too large. When did he start looking so old?

I search for something to say, ask him if the shop's been busy these days, think about the craters under his eyes, tell him he should think about retiring soon. He asks me if I've been eating enough fruit lately, asks me how my dissertation is going, laughs and says he still doesn't understand what his daughter does, but trusts that it's important. I tell him that I've been eating fruit every night and the dissertation is moving along, albeit slowly. I tell him I should defend by the end of the year. I don't tell him that my doctor just increased my Zoloft dosage, or that these days, I sleep under two hours every night, tossing and turning with a bad, unidentifiable feeling in my gut.

Our words over dinner carry themselves as they always have, presenting half versions of ourselves. We don't ever say much about her. We don't actively avoid the topic; we've simply acknowledged her absence as fact, the way our lives are now, had been for a long time.

After dinner, I help do the dishes, and my dad chops a few apples up for us to snack on. He's still not convinced that I'm eating enough fruit. We bring our heaping plates of fruit to the living room, sit on the couch, and my dad pulls out his new iPad, tells me he's having trouble logging into his e-mail. I explain that it should be the same as his desktop, but go ahead and take the gadget from him, offering to help. I sit cross-legged, put the iPad on my lap. *I need your password before I can do anything*, I tell him, as he hovers over my shoulder. He leans over and types the four-digit password on the home screen, and I can't help but be nosy and watch. I replay the digits in my head. It's a month and day, I realize. It's my mother's birthday, I realize. I look at my dad, who looks unfazed, taking a bite of apple, waiting for me to carry out the next step to help him figure out his email.

And I realize that there is a ghost that haunts my father. She always has. He may rarely talk about her, but he nods to her, continues grieving, in small ways. He carries her with him, gently; she lives in our house, continues to sleep on their bed, sits with him at the kitchen table; her memories dig craters under his eyes. I think back to the day we unloaded the bags of my mother's clothing at the Salvation Army. Realize that a spindly nine year-old isn't much help in carrying a couple garbage bags of clothes out of a car and into a building. Realize that perhaps, my dad just didn't want to do it alone.

21

DISPATCHES FROM NOWHERE BY KAWAI SHEN

It may be true that a Canadian Born Chinese (CBC) can never fully belong as a Canadian or a Chinese person, but this is only a partial view. The inversion of this claim is that a CBC is also not fully excluded from either group. Therein lies the key to understanding a CBC.

I don't exist outside of two discrete categories as implied by the pejorative Cantonese term, *jook sing mui*, which translates roughly to "bamboo girl." This term positions foreign-born Chinese in between two disconnected bamboo segments, unable to connect to either "world." Yet it is also not accurate to say that I exist within the two categories as suggested by terms like banana. Such terms presume that my identity can be split into tidy ratios, as if my yellow Chinese skin could conceal a white Canadian within. Nor do I perfectly synthesize east and west in some kind of celebratory, multicultural mosaic, for these ideas are founded upon the assumption that race and nationality are more stable than they actually are. They are inadequate models that fail to capture how CBCs can deftly navigate a world of shifting categories.

How many second generation Canadians have been sold a narrative of exclusion and internal conflict? How many were taught to measure out their identities in fractions — a few Chinese points for speaking

Cantonese or taking Kumon lessons, a few Canadian points for watching MuchMusic or eating Kraft Dinner — only to find out those fractions never added up to a whole?

How many CBCs have acted as their own internalized immigration officers, racking up Chinese and Canadian points to gain status in the mythological states of national and racial identity?

I refuse to police boundaries that make no sense to me. It is not racial and national categories that are stable and complete while I am the one who is torn between two worlds. I'm feeling just fine, thank you. No, I'm the one who is intact while these categories are riddled with holes.

I understand the desire to situate CBCs in relation to categorical boundaries. I understand the need to pin me on a map because it is so much harder to figure out what one's relationship is to a moving target. But CBCs cannot be confined to one place; they are constantly renegotiating their position in relation to the boundaries society would have defined.

"They know I'm from Canada, but I speak Japanese. And then they don't know what to do with me," a former boss once told me. He was a nisei, a second generation Japanese-Canadian, who conducted business regularly in Japan."There's a space that opens up between what they expect and who I am." And what we do with this space, is our choice.

Terms like jook sing mui and banana taught me that the CBC category was a passive, negative space formed in between the positive spaces of Chinese and Canadian. I am more interested in the space my former boss described. It is dynamic, full of potential, and defies being affixed to anything. Unable to remain safely ensconced within the boundaries of national and racial identity, I grew up playing in unclassifiable spaces of possibilities and movement that still continually open up before me. This can be disorienting, but also liberating. For the ability to fully inhabit the space between what is imagined and what is real, and to exercise agency within this space, are skills that can be learned.

We can practice skills that challenge the distance between expectations and lived experiences; contracting to become disarming and to put others at ease, or expanding to unsettle, just as my former boss used his fluent Japanese to destabilize others to his advantage in business negotiations. Instead of passively waiting for others to classify me, instead of sitting obediently in that spot, I can subtly guide others with my body language or word choice into placing me where I wish to be. When external pressures like the question, "Where are you really from?" or terms like jook sing mui threaten to collapse or solidify this space, we can train ourselves to reopen it and destabilize it again.

While applying these skills on others, CBCs can also apply them to themselves. Instead of merely assimilating, I carry this space to make myself welcome wherever I happen to be. In this way, I have carried the confidence to enter somewhere uninvited and do it in plain view. I now recognize that when I'm the only Asian in the room, or the only Canadian native, I can take it upon myself to take up more space for myself. And I will make myself comfortable as someone who can belong without belonging.

Instead of simply seeking protection or meaning from boundaries that can never circumscribe lived experiences, I propose learning to relish one's freedom from them and to value the ability to transgress imperfect categories. How much easier it is for a CBC to cross the line when she is willing to embrace the chaos and contingency of existing in the here and now. How much easier it is for me to evade capture when everyone else is still looking at the wrong maps, maps with clear, discrete borders demarcating imaginary territories. I am not like you, but I am also not not like you; now catch me if you can.

Because it's almost always the case that the lines I'm crossing are only being crossed in someone else's head. And because by the time someone realizes that there's something not quite right about me, that I don't fully belong, I'm already somewhere else. In fact, if you think about it, I was never really there.

22

CONFESSION OF A CATHOLIC'S DAUGHTER AT THE TEMPLE OF AU CO, THIRTY-FIVE YEARS POST-EXODUS BY DO NGUYEN MAI

Save me, Mother, for I am burning.

We became water / Father
devoured our hearts to build a kingdom
drowned the earth to suffocate all embers,
but our hearths, scraped dry by the salt, flooded with
mouths gaping, empty, gasping. Will our boats float
upon this sea of fire? *Mẹ ơi, có nhớ con là ai không?*

Once, my name was *Mai* but then
it was *Mei & Marie & Mia* and
Han Dynasty & Indochine & Vietnam War and

now our boats sink, heavy with unknown bodies,
dropped into the inescapable belly of firestorm —
we think this is hell but it is your womb;
we know you to be light but we believe you are ruin.

For how many lives have I wronged you, Mother?

Mẹ có biết con là ai không? Tell me I still have a heart.
Tell me I did not give up my name to become
the ocean, which only disappears in the face of flame.
Tell me I did not leave only to be consumed by the yearning.
Tell me I am still kindling and not ash.

Mother, free me from the drowning.

Mother, remember me.

23

A COLLECTION OF ROOMS BY EMI KODAMA

In your house, the lights turn on and off in different directions. Some switches flip up to turn on, others flip down to turn on. There's a bank of five switches in the living room: to turn on the lamp by the couch, the lights in the ceiling, the spotlight in the display case, the fixture above the table, and the hall light. Although the switches point in different directions, there is a logic to them. They create a map of the lights in the room. I didn't realize this until much later.

Before you start up the stairs to the first floor, you can switch on the hall light upstairs. And when you get to the first floor, you can switch off the hall light on the ground floor. Light switches guide you through the house. One on, the next off, so that you're never standing in the dark. We've never met in darkness.

There was this year when we had thirty straight days of rain in November, and we never saw the sun. Or the moon. Afterwards, you climbed the roof and installed a ten-meter pole with a globe lamp attached to it. It hangs above your little garden, and sometimes you go out to look at it in the middle of the night.

On those nights, the neighbourhood seems unusually quiet, and the outline of my window becomes a picture frame.

We are sitting outside, even though the chairs are damp. I wrap the blanket around me a little tighter.

"Good thing is, there are two more minutes of daylight every day," I say.

"Oh! What is that, like the length of time it takes to make a sandwich?"

I think for a moment. "Or brush your teeth," I say.

"It's just long enough to look around and smile," you say.

With your hands in your pockets, you're doing just that. "What are you so smiley about?" I ask.

You shrug. "I'm having a good hair day."

"That is something to be happy about."

"And it's almost your birthday," you say.

"Really? When?"

"On Tuesday."

By then, we could be surrounded by snow. The night sky will take on a purple hue, and the city will come to a standstill. On your birthday, the tulips were out. It was warm enough to ride your bike without a jacket.

Tonight, there are two moons. One is full. The other is not. One temporarily hides behind a cloud. The other remains radiant. We stay here just long enough to see one moon float past the other.

One always knows where the other is in the house. Your bedroom's on the second floor, but I can hear you cough when I sit with a cup of tea in the living room. You hear me on the phone with my sister. You ask me later how she's doing.

At first I searched for a lock on the bathroom door, but realized there is none because you can always tell if there's someone inside by the light coming through the frosted glass.

It's like living in a house without walls. I think of you standing in the grass and remember we have met once in the dark. Once, when I blindly flicked switches and plunged us into darkness momentarily. In the dark, you were an afterimage burned on my retina, and you seemed doubled, as I saw you a split-second later in the light.

"I've been noticing time go by really fast lately," I say.

"But there's plenty of it," you reply.

"Yeah, I forget that sometimes."

We're sitting outside. You've recently put out the garden furniture again. The soil seems ready to grow things.

On most mornings, I look at a weather cam image from back home. There is a new photo every fifteen minutes until the sun goes down. At sundown, it is the middle of rush hour. Headlights line the bridge. It is the last photo of the previous day and the image I often wake up to because of the time difference. And so it seems that yesterday stretches into today. That night stretches into day. That the lights dotting the horizon there continue to burn as the sun scales the sky here.

I imagine someone like you, climbing the roof to clean the lens on a fine spring day.

You glance at your watch. "Like there's still a hundred and eighty minutes left of today — give or take."

"I don't think I've ever seen you wear a watch."

"It's new. See how useful it is? It even lights up." You hold up your wrist.

"Nice. I'm a fan of anything that makes life easier. Life is hard, don't you think?"

You look at me sideways."Only a little."

"I knew you'd say that."

You are walking around in a T-shirt like it's the middle of summer.

"Well, I guess you're on easy street when your birthday's tomorrow."

"Tomorrow? That's still ages away."

"And what are you going to do with all that time?"

"Oh, I dunno... Whip up a gourmet meal. Alphabetize my books. Maybe dye my hair a fun colour."

I laugh. "I guess the possibilities are endless."

The morning is slightly overcast. I count one, two, three patches of blue sky. The day is just about to begin.

"Is there something you really want but don't have yet?" I ask.

You are leaning against the railing, looking out across the water.

Your T-shirt flaps in the wind.

"I'd say there are things that I look forward to, like travelling and owning a farm... having a family... Being old."

"Being old?"

"Yeah, like all the life experiences I would have. All that wisdom."

When you turn your face, your voice almost disappears in the sound of the engine. It's been almost half an hour since we left the harbor.

"Do you feel like you're getting wiser?" I ask.

"I wish I could feel it on a day-to-day basis, but sometimes, it hits you suddenly. Like I'll look back and see that I've changed a lot." You scratch your shoulder. "You?"

"I realize how unwise I actually am, and it's like I was just too naïve to notice before." I wiggle my toes in my shoes. "I've never looked forward to being old."

"Why not?"

The wind has turned your hair into a cloud above your head.

"Like imagine being seventy-seven, and realizing that this might be the last time you're here in this very spot. It's been really fun but also exhausting, and you don't think you'll have the energy for it – ever again. And I'm talking about the conscious understanding of that because lots of things could be your last time without you knowing it." I press my eyes with my palms. They burn.

We left in the semi-darkness to make it to the ferry on time. You unlocked the car, and your door slammed shut before mine. The sky grew bright over the mountains as we drove. Even at that early hour, it was noticeably cooler in the shade than in the light. The windows on both sides were open.

"What would you say if you knew this was the last conversation we were ever going to have?" I ask.

"That's a tough one." You rest your chin on your hand.

Last night, you wanted to stay up until the sun came up. You suggested it like it was the best idea you'd ever had.

"Maybe we would just reminisce about the old times," you say.

"Like a summary of all the important things?" I quickly try to think of all the important things. "I guess it would be too late for anything new."

The patches of blue sky are slowly shifting, and the forecast for rain seems to be fading.

"I just hate that feeling of knowing that something is your last time," I say.

"There need to be endings so that new things can start."

"I'm trying to sort through all my junk." I pull on my hood. "I started having this funny feeling that I'm blind to my surroundings. Like if I think about what's under my bed, I have no idea."

"I can relate to that."

I turn towards you."It makes your whole space smaller, don't you think?"

"But I like it, going through old boxes and being surprised. It's like finding something you forgot you lost." Your voice is as bright as your eyes.

"Or like being a fish who thinks he's swimming in an endless ocean, when really, his memory resets every time he makes the next round in the tank."

"Is that sad or lucky?"

"I think it's both." I bend down and grab a granola bar from my backpack. I took too long in the shower this morning and only had time for a small breakfast. Half-awake, I felt like I was standing in a lagoon under a pounding waterfall. I might have heard birds.

"Do you want a snack?" I ask. "Maybe later."

I take a bite.

"Sometimes I'm tempted to throw everything away without going through any of it," you say. "To just set it all out on the curb. Wouldn't that feel good?"

You would break a sweat carrying all your stuff up the driveway. I imagine you coming home in the evening to find it all gone. I think about my drafts of letters, maps people have drawn me, lists, clippings, ticket stubs — all making my drawers difficult to open.

"I probably wouldn't miss most of it since I only look at it when I'm cleaning," I say. "But oh, I don't think I could ever just get rid of it all."

"Just in case?"

"Just in case."

The ocean is nearly the same colour until the horizon. We might see whales.

"So what about you? What do you want?" you ask.

"I've been thinking about that, and I can't come up with anything."

"Nothing?"

"I mean, how can you know you want something if you've never had it before?" I wave my granola bar around for emphasis. "So maybe I want more of what I already have. Like I want my good friends to become better friends. Keep working on my own stuff. Keep travelling. Go farther. And have new things come out of that." I shrug.

"So it means you're happy with what you have. That's good," you say. "But I think we often want what we've never had before. Probably a gift and a curse at the same time."

"Sometimes I feel too easily influenced. Like I just want what the cool kids have."

"I think we're all susceptible to that. Weren't you one of the cool kids in school?"

"Are you kidding?" I frown."I was a goody two-shoes."

You try to hide a smile. "I think you probably just wanted to do your best."

"When I was little, I had to look perfect before I left the house. Like my braids had to be smooth and even, my shirt had to be tucked in just right, and my socks had to be pulled up properly."

You laugh. "I just got a mental image of a little you standing in front of the mirror."

When I look at old photos of myself, I feel like I haven't changed as much as my sister has. Sometimes I like that. Sometimes I don't.

"What happened if everything wasn't perfect?" you ask.

"It would be a bad start to the day and I'd feel uncomfortable." My scarf unfurls in the wind.

"I bet your socks didn't even match."

"I won't deny it. Maybe a shirt without a button."

"And look at you now, a free spirit," I say.

"And what are you?"

"That's a good question."

The sun appears like the moon through the clouds. I look at it directly. "After a while, I realized that getting ready made me really anxious, so I started having 'imperfect days' where I'd just throw on my clothes and comb my hair really fast," I say.

"And did you feel better after that?"

"It bothered me at first, but I eventually got used to it and I did feel better, so I started having more imperfect days until all my days were that way."

You lean back and put your hands in your pockets. You look at the ground. "You know, there's only one of you so you're fine the way you are."

"Chaplin once won third prize in a Charlie Chaplin look-alike contest." You shake your head. "Poor guy."

It occurs to me that I'm only minorly happy that we didn't stay up all night.

"When we were talking about getting old, I forgot to say that I hope I know you for a really long time," I say.

"Me too."

"Maybe there will be so many fun times we won't be able to remember them all."

"I'll help you remember," you say. "That's friendly."

I watch a propeller at the top of the ferry turn steadily. I point to it. "What is that?"

"Radar. To detect other boats and objects in the water." "Oh! And to signal its own location, I guess."

"Yeah. Seeing is to be seen," you say. The sky behind it is blue.

The sun breaks through the clouds, and the ferry casts a shadow on the water. It ripples over the surface in cobalt blue. On the deck, there are two small figures. I wave and the silhouette waves back. As I continue to watch, I get the impression that the shadow is actually a vessel underwater, travelling at the same speed as us. On board, its two passengers are also pointing, wondering — marvelling at an entirely different world to theirs.

My sister has a small projector that shines constellations around her room. She got it as a birthday present, and I always wanted one of my own. The stars turn slowly, and it's as if the earth has somehow speeded up. It came with a book that explained the star systems, and we used to study it carefully with a flashlight.

My sister is very good at recognizing constellations in the night sky, whereas I am not. In the real sky, there are so many more stars than were projected on her ceiling.

Back at the house, there are still fewer visible stars. It never really gets dark in the city. I wonder if my sister still has that projector. I've gotten you one for your birthday.

When you turn it on, the universe shrinks to the size of your bedroom. All four seasons pass in one evening. On sleepless nights, it seems that the earth is turning faster, that day will come sooner, and you, just another star among millions, are floating towards the sun.

"I think I may have chosen the wrong day to do this," you say. There is only one tree in the yard and you are sitting in it, untangling a string of Christmas lights. The wind has been picking up steadily in the last hour, and you are bobbing up and down on a branch as if you were moored to a buoy. I slide the door closed behind me as I step outside. Your hair whips in the breeze.

"Maybe you should come down before you get seasick," I say.

"Almost... Got it!" you say, as the last few lights unravel. You secure the end to the tree, and I hold the ladder as you climb down.

"Wait, we can't go in until we see the fruits of my labour," you say. You pick up the plug and hold it to the socket. "Ready?"

"Unleash the magic!" I say.

The lights only illuminate the bottom half of the tree and burn against the blue-gray sky.

Your face lights up. Clouds skim the sky.

"I think today was the perfect day to hang them," I say.

The lights sway to and fro, open, upwards, ready to catch whatever may tumble down towards us.

24

THE GARDENER BY LISA ZHANG

i heard from my mother that
i must be a complete person
before i can love.
well, i have been an architect.
i have poured concrete for years,
and i have a brutal building
that looks built to last.
that's a mistake —
to try to outlast life.
i will never be whole.
for all my learning,
i know less than socrates
but I do know this:
you deserve something that grows —
let us be gardeners.

i want to love you in a tangle of vines —
i'll peer through the mess of green
and there you'll be, okay with me as I am —
as I cry inside a fleece like a child

or cut down enemies with my mother's tongue.

let us tend to our garden each day.
each night,
there's the routine:
the light of a little lamp for us to share.
we sleep in a small jungle
until i am in dreamland —
you are senseless till morning

25

HOMECOMING BY HANNAH POLINSKI

Thanksgiving dinner at my grandparents' house consists of turkey, mashed potatoes, cranberries, rice, broccoli with fungus, glass noodles with bean curd, and Tofurkey. My Gung Gung cooks all afternoon in silence, shuffling slowly around the kitchen in his blue slippers. My Poh Poh watches Chinese soap operas in the living room, the volume turned up loud enough so Gung Gung can hear the voices over the chop of his knife on the wood cutting board. Occasionally she will come up for a plate of fruit and ask a few questions about the meal, to which Gung Gung will wave his hands and grumble back in Cantonese. Patting her dyed black hair, she will return to the television and call one of our many relatives.

We arrive at five o'clock like we do every year. If we are even a minute late, Poh Poh calls our house to remind us that we are eating soon, even though she had called ten minutes previously. We arrive as Poh Poh brings the steaming dishes smelling of savoury meats to the table, barely leaving any room for our plates and bowls of rice. I sit below a black and white headshot of my Bak Bak, my great-grandmother, old enough that the photo must have been taken in

Canada but young enough that I do notrecognize the sea of grey hair that sits atop her head.

I have been a vegetarian for six years now but every meal we eat together, my grandparents point to the dishes and indicate which have meat or not. I'm reaching for the gravy when Poh Poh motions towards the bowl of broccoli.

"Broccoli have no meat," she declares. "I know."

"Mhm."

I wouldn't say our dinners are silent. The sound of chopsticks scraping rice bowls and soup slurped on large white spoons echoes, while sentences started as hands reach for second helpings that lay scattered across the table.

"I'm moving to South Korea next year," I say, putting my fork down.

Gung Gung nods while Poh Poh's chopsticks entrap a brain-like piece of bean curd.

"Korea not safe. They communist in Korea," Poh Poh says shaking her head.

"Ai," says Gung Gung. "That's North."

"Oh. You no go to North." She continues to shake her head.

"You can't even get into North Korea!" My mom yells and shakes her head in unison with my Poh Poh, although for a different reason.

二

I'm not at home much anymore. Christmas, Thanksgiving, and the two reading weeks my university affords me are the only times I make it back to my quiet town. But every time I am back, I try to learn a little more about my family history. I'm not sure what prompts this desire in me. Maybe it is the way I have to shout a little louder each time I see Gung Gung. Maybe it is overhearing Poh Poh and her sister discussing their medications as if they were trading cards. Maybe it is enrolling in Mandarin classes at school and remembering that I never had a conversation with Bak Bak when she was alive.

My family never helps with cleaning up, especially not my brother or father who naturally gravitate towards watching football in the living room. If I try to help, Poh Poh takes the dirty plates from my hands.

Instead I sit in the kitchen with its grease coated cupboards, spending an hour in the kitchen half-yelling questions to my increasingly deaf grandparents. *How old were you? What year was it?* Gung Gung is nine years older than Poh Poh but arrived in Canada in 1953. Poh Poh came later in 1960. *How did you know each other?*

"Poh Poh was a mail order bride," my mom says from the dining room while flipping through pages of the Toronto Star. "Or maybe it was Aunt Mary. I think one of them was."

I search for "Chinese mail order wife" on my phone and expect to see a Wikipedia page followed by scholarly articles and intersectional feminist essays. Instead I am led to page after page of websites among the likes of My New Chinese Wife, Sincere Asian Brides, and China Love Cupid.

"My brother know Gung Gung from China," Poh Poh says as Gung Gung boils water for tea."We write letters to each other and I come to Canada."

"See?" My mom smirks into the paper.

三

Bak Bak died nine years ago at the age of 101. Near the end of her life she used to dig in the front yard of Gung Gung and Poh Poh's house. Thinking she had returned to China, she dug for the valuables that she had buried the day she fled Canton with only her children. Sometimes they found her with dirt lodged under her fingernails and mud crusted on her jade bracelets. Unless it had rained the night before, the ground was usually too hard for her frail body to crack, leaving her knees and hands dusty as she struggled to get back to her feet. Other times they came home to her circling the bushes that lined the sidewalk, searching for the right spot as she asked herself aloud where her husband was.

On several occasions she left the house alone without a sense of what country she was in. Dressed in layers of oversized sweaters and patterned Chinese jackets, she shuffled along the sidewalks in her red slippers. Kind strangers jumped out into the middle of traffic to help her across the street when she crossed at places with no pedestrian signs, oblivious to the honks of angry drivers. Speaking no English, the only sound she made came from the pebbles that scraped the pavement beneath her feet.

As soon as someone realized she was missing, Gung Gung got in his car and drove around the neighbourhood. Poh Poh wandered the streets looking for her century-old mother, and usually found her down by the river. After several "escapes", my grandparents installed what my mother dubbed "the Bak Bak lock", several complicated locks on the front door that she struggled to open.

I don't know the Cantonese word for great-grandfather because I've never had to use it. Nobody in my family knows what became of Poh Poh's father. All we've been told is that he "died fleeing communist China".

四

Poh Poh places the leftovers in plastic containers, ranging from actual Tupperware to empty margarine tubs. Gung Gung runs a toothpick through his teeth as his blue slippers shuffle into the living room to watch football.

"Why did you come to Canada? How did you get here? But why Canada, what was wrong with Macau?" I ask, growing exasperated by Poh Poh's answers.

"We were from Canton," Poh Poh doesn't pause as she continues sweeping the kitchen."We paid a lot of money to go to Macau."

Macau. A city that has eluded me but lays one Google search away. I've asked about Macau many times to both Poh Poh and my Chinese friends and they all like to laugh and say it is the *Lahsy Veghasy — Las Vegas* — of China.

She leaves the kitchen to fetch a broom from the garage."Poh Poh isn't very good at this." I complain and scroll on my phone, listening to the football announcer's muffled voice. My mother sits in the dining room with the photo of Bak Bak looking over her, reading the paper with a concentration that does not suggest her knowledge of our family history, neither her refusal to share it with me.

五

I used to work at a clothing boutique on Toronto's hip Queen St. West owned by a Chinese lady from Hong Kong. She learned quickly to roll her eyes at the young girls who tried haggling over a few dollars for a t-shirt. When the store wasn't busy, she sent me to pick up mushroom rice for her in Chinatown. On my first rice run, I entered the restaurant as a white family was walking out.

"They're all so rude," the father shook his head without holding the door for the customers behind him. "And the chicken balls weren't even authentic."

Inside the restaurant a thin girl wearing a Hello Kitty shirt, no older than 12, sat at the counter between a gold paw-waving cat figurine and fake jade Buddha. Her hair framed the sides of her face as she added up a bill on a stained calculator, oblivious to the waiters shouting behind her.

The Chinese Diaspora. Generations of immigration embodied by Chinese restaurants known best to their customers for fortune cookies and sweet and sour pork, both creations to satisfy the fork-wielding customer. The restaurant itself takes on the role of a parent, nurturing the immigrant child to grow to pursue the life it never had.

These are the children who grow up knowing the length of bus and subway trips rather than one-way boat rides. They have never buried their family heirlooms under thick layers of clay and left everything in another hemisphere. They may ask their grandparents their stories, but they fail when the conversations are held, in Gung Gung's case, in a language learned at the age of 19 in a Canadian sixth-grade classroom.

Later that day I cried reading Amy Tan's *The Joy Luck Club.* It doesn't seem to be a coincidence that her main character's parents came from Guangzhou and Toishan, like my grandparents did. I felt something tightening inside my chest that was not guilt exactly, nor was it sympathy. The same night I read a poem by Nayyirah Waheed. *"you broke the ocean in/half to be here/only to meet nothing that wants you."* I was not prepared to confront the fact that this nothingness could come from your own bloodline.

六

She comes back into the kitchen and puts the broom in the corner. She washes her hands in the sink and turns towards the fridge, but stops right in front of my stool.

"We paid a lot to go to Macau," she repeats.

Macau: located in the south approximately 64 kilometers from Hong Kong. Under control by the Portuguese from the 16th century until 1999. The longest European-controlled colony in Asia. Officially part of China but an autonomous territory, Macau is one of the richest regions in the world. Home to the largest gambling centre and the fourth highest life expectancy rate in the world. The Lahsy-Veghasy of China.

"In Canton we got on boat," Poh Poh extends her arms their full span, not even covering the full length of the fridge and the stove. "Very small. 6 of us: me, Bak Bak, Uncle Mike, Aunt Lucy, Uncle Tom, Uncle Tom's wife." She lifts her arms again."We lay down in the boat and put sugar cane on top of us so they can't see us. We hiding. We so scared. There are two men rowing the boat. They say, 'if the soldiers find us they kill us. Throw us into the water. We drown.' I didn't hear but my mother and Uncle Tom hear. We so scared. They shaking. We rowing then we stop and police boat passes by. Many times. The police boat look but only see sugar cane so they keep rowing. They think it is just supplies. We thought we would die. Then we see lights of Macau on the water. So happy! They say 'only half hours more'. I was so happy. We thought we would die. We paid a lot of money to go to Macau."

I don't notice I'm pinching my arm until I feel the moon-shaped indents in my skin a few minutes later. Poh Poh is looking at me, her dark eyes glistening, not with tears, but with a look I've never seen before.

"How old were you?" I say after a moment of silence.

"I was 10. Maybe 11." She walks over to the fridge and continues putting away the Thanksgiving meal.

I wonder what her story would have been like had I been able to speak her language. Cantonese, the ancestral tongue that skipped my generation, only grazing my mother's. English seems like a trap, molding her experiences into verbs and adjectives she can barely pronounce.

In the dining room, my mother continues to flip pages of the newspaper as if she hasn't heard anything at all.

七

Last week I met up with a boy from my university who had returned from two years teaching abroad in Korea. I told him I was interested in doing the same, and while chewing the tapioca pearls of bubble tea he asked me why I wouldn't go to China first. China, the place where front yards can double as treasure hunts. China, the place where the language is familiar to my ears yet I cannot pick out a single word. China, the place my family almost died to escape.

I didn't explain why I'm not moving to China. He took no notice, rattling on about how beautiful Asia was with all its gorgeous women. I soon excused myself and never spoke to him again.

八

Poh Poh climbed out of the small rowboat on the shore of Macau at the age of eleven. Indents from the mound of sugar cane piled high on top of her and her sister's boots were imprinted in red on her fair skin. She took several deep breaths, smelling fish in the air as she stretched her arms towards the black sky. The six of them smoothed out their layers of clothing and trekked into the darkness towards the city where they had a one-bedroom apartment on the third floor waiting for them.

The next day, Bak Bak hired a detective to find her husband. He had left Canton six months prior to their own crossing to ensure the route was safe enough for them to follow. Poh Poh thought that perhaps he had settled down as an elegant bachelor in the heart of Macau, spending his Friday nights betting on *mah jong* and his Saturday nights taking different women out for dinner. Or maybe he had buried himself under sugar cane on the wrong boat and emerged hours after pushing off the shores of Canton into the dazzling lights of the San Francisco harbour. They never heard from him again.

26

ABOUT OUR CONTRIBUTORS

Aaron Tang was born in Vancouver, and went to Hong Kong at the age of five, where he attended school for nine years before returning to Canada to attend High School and University. After graduating from Queen's University in the summer of 2016 with a Bachelor's Degree in Film, he decided to attend the University of Guelph for a Master's of Fine Arts in Creative Writing.

Aileen Santos is a Filipina-Canadian writer and high school teacher in the Greater Toronto Area. Her debut novel, *Someone Like You*, was published May 2016 by Two Wolves Press. Her creative non-fiction piece, Six, is forthcoming Spring 2017 in the anthology, *Wherever I Find Myself: Stories by Canadian Immigrant Women* published by Caitlin Press.

Born and raised in Beijing, China, **Anna Wang Yuan** had authored four novels and one short story collection in Chinese before she immigrated to Canada in 2006. Her short story collection *Beijing Women: Stories* was published by Merwin Asia in 2014. She translated Alice Munro's *The View from Castle Rock* into Chinese in 2015.

Benjamin Hertwig's first book of poems, *Slow War*, is coming out with McGill-Queen's in 2017. His writing has recently appeared or is forthcoming on *NPR*, in the *New York Times, THIS, Word Riot,Prairie Fire, Freefall, Matrix, Qwerty,* and *Geez*. He lives in Vancouver, on the unceded land of the Musqueam, Squamish and Tsleil-Waututh First Nations.

Carousel Calvo is a Filipino-Canadian writer currently living in Vancouver, BC. She has published her works at *Ricepaper, Prairie Fire, Lyre, Headlight Anthology*, and *Soliloquies*.

Céline Chuang is a multidisciplinary creative and proud, if often culturally confused, descendent of the Chinese-Mauritian diaspora. She slings espresso by day, freelances graphic design by night, reads voraciously, and sleeps in whenever possible. She lives in Vancouver.

Cheonhak Kwon debuted through the Contemporary Literature in South Korea. She immigrated to Canada in 2008, and was awarded the Kyung Hee University Overseas Korean Literary Award (Grand Prize) in 2010 for the short story *Stuffed Cucumber Kimchi* and the Distinguished Poet Award in 2015 by Writers International Network Canada. The translations of Kwon's poetry received the Harvard University's Translation Award and the 41st Korea Times Modern Korean Literature Award.

Hana Kim is the Director of Cheng Yu Tung East Asian Library, at the University of Toronto. In her time away from work, she enjoys translating the work of her mother, Cheonhak Kwon. One of her major translated publications is $2H_2 + O_2 = 2H_2O$ (2011). This translation won the Sunshik Min Prize of the Min Chapbook Competition from Harvard University's Korean Institute and Tamal Vista Publications.

John Mokrynskyj worked as a translator and interpreter for Korean, Japanese, Chinese, Ukrainian and Russian and is currently the Japanese Specialist at the University of Toronto. John Mokrynskyj and Hana Kim are recipients of the Korea Times' 41st Modern Korean Literature Translation Awards — Poetry Division Commendation Award.

Do Nguyen Mai — name written family name to given name — is a Vietnamese American poet currently residing in Los Angeles, and she is the founder and editor-in-chief of *Rambutan Literary*. Her debut poetry collection, *Ghosts Still Walking*, is available from Platypus Press.

Dung Kai-cheung is a Chinese fiction writer born in Hong Kong. As an author, journalist, playwright and essayist, Dung is a part-time lecturer at The Chinese University of Hong Kong and mainly teaches Chinese writing. His most important novels include *Atlas* and *Histories of Time*. Different from other local Chinese writers, Dung translates his own work into English versions. Dung is devoted to the education of youth writers. He writes preface and prologue for Hong Kong youth writers, some of whom are his students in the Chinese department of Chinese University of Hong Kong.

Nick Stember now works as *Ricepaper Magazine*'s translation editor.

Originally from Vancouver, **Emi Kodama** is a visual artist who has been living in Ghent, Belgium since 2008. She has an MFA from the Frank Mohr Institute in Groningen (NL). Her first collection of short stories and drawings *If I Were You* was published by MER. Paper Kunsthalle in 2012.

Frances Du is a poet and photographer based in Toronto, Ontario. Her work has been published in the *Hart House Review* and *The Literary Review of Canada*. She is currently working on her first book of poems, *PORTRAITS*. You can connect with her @frannywrites.

Hannah Polinski is a writer and undergraduate student in her fourth year of the BA English program at Ryerson University. She is currently based in Toronto and her work has appeared in local publications such as *The Continuist*.

Helen Tran is poet and novelist who recently graduated from UBC with an MFA in Creative Writing. Her thesis project was a steampunk novel written under the supervision of Joseph Boyden. She is a professor of communications at Niagara College, and enjoys teaching creative writing at Centauri Summer Arts camp.

Jane Aiko Komori's "Japanese Cheese" draws on her experiences living in the BC Interior. Her work has appeared in several publications, including *GUTS Canadian Feminist Magazine* and a forthcoming piece in *Matrix Magazine*. Originally from Kamloops, BC, Jane is a gender, sexuality, and women's studies student at Simon Fraser University and currently pursues writing, academics, and activist work in Vancouver.

Born in Singapore, raised in Suzhou and Hong Kong, **Jasmine Gui** currently lives and works in Toronto. She is the Founder of Project 40 Collective, and the Managing Editor at *LooseLeaf magazine*. Her poetry has been published by *Hart House Review, text, Acta Victoriana, Red Paint Hill,* (parenthetical), and more. She writes at jaziimun.com.

JF Garrard is the founder of Dark Helix Press, Co-President of Canadian Authors Association's Toronto Branch, Deputy Editor for *Ricepaper Magazine*, Festival Coordinator for LiterASIAN (Toronto) and Assistant Editor for *Amazing Stories* magazine. Her latest stories include "The Curse" in the *Brave New Girls: Adventures of Gales and Gizmos* anthology, "The Metamorphosis of Nova" in the *Blood Is Thicker* anthology by Iguana Books and "The Perfect Husband" in the *We Shall Be Monsters Frankenstein* anthology by Renaissance Press. Visit her website jfgarrard.com for more details.

Joanne Leow is an Assistant Professor in the Department of English at the University of Saskatchewan. Her poetry and creative non-fiction have been published in *Catapult Magazine, Quarterly Literary Review of Singapore, Little Things: An Anthology of Poetry* (Ethos Books), and the now defunct *Junoesq*. She grew up in Singapore.

Kawai Shen is a Canadian Born Chinese writer and cartoonist based in

Toronto. You can find her online at cutejuicecomics.com or as @kawaishen on Twitter.

Li Charmaine Anne grew up and writes on the unceded territory of the Musqueam. She is an undergraduate student in the University of British Columbia Creative Writing Program. Her writing focuses on the intersections between identity, music, and growing up on the Pacific Northwest. Read more about her website, breakfastwithwords.wordpress.com.

Linda Nguyen earned her M.F.A. in Creative Writing from Wilkes University and her B.A. in Psychology from McGill University. She now works in the video game industry on AAA titles. Born in Winnipeg, she lives in Montréal where her mind wanders and her fingers type.

Lisa Zhang is a doctoral student in clinical psychology at the University of British Columbia. Her work deals with perfectionism and its effects on psychotherapy. When not writing academic articles, she writes fiction and poetry.

Mary Chen is a queer Chinese Canadian artist and writer who has grown up in the cradle of unceded Coast Salish land. She is currently completing a BFA in Creative Writing at the University of British Columbia and has previously been published in *Looseleaf* literary magazine.

Raine Ling is a Chinese-Canadian writer interested in exploring how loneliness and suffering exists within families, across generational and cultural lines. She is currently based out of Toronto, Ontario.

Stanford Cheung is a poet, writer, and musician from Toronto, Scarborough. He published his first poetry collection in 2014. His chapbook *Any Seam or Needlework* was released by The Operating System Press in 2016 as part of their Of Sound Mind Series. A Pushcart Prize nominee, his work, notes, and drafts appear in *Nomadic Journal: Changes III, X-Peri Magazine, Ex-ex Literature, Zoomoozophone Review* and elsewhere. He currently studies at the University of Toronto.

Zeng Xiaowen has published three novels — *The Daytime Floating Journey, The Night Is Still Young* and *The Immigrant Years*; a collection of short stories and novellas — *The Kilt and Clover*; a collection of prose — *Turn Your Back to the Moon*; and more than three hundred other short stories, pieces of prose, poems, and essays. Her works have been included in a number of literature collections. The short story, *The Kilt and Clover,* was on the China Fiction Association's Top 10 List for 2009. Further, she co-wrote and published, with Sun Bo, a 20-episode TV drama *Invented in China*, which won a Chinese Writers Erduosi Literature Award and a Zhongshan Cup Overseas Chinese Literature Award in 2011. It has recently been made into a 33-episode series re-titled *Let Go of Your Hand.*

Alison Bailey is a professor in the Asian Studies Department at the University of British Columbia.

"WE CAN DO ANYTHING"

A.C.W.W

27

ABOUT OUR TEAM

Allan Cho: Executive Editor

Allan Cho is the Executive Editor of *Ricepaper Magazine*, and is an academic librarian at the University of British Columbia. Allan is actively engaged in a number of initiatives in the community, and serves on the board of the Asian Canadian Writers' Workshop and Vancouver Asian Heritage Month Society. He has written for the *Georgia Straight, Diverse Magazine*, and *Ricepaper*. His fiction has appeared in the anthologies, *The Strangers* and *Eating Stories*. He is one of the founders of LiterASIAN Writers Festival and is a co-editor of the anthology, *AlliterAsian: Celebrating Twenty Years of Ricepaper Magazine.*

Karla Comanda: Fiction Editor

Karla Comanda is *Ricepaper Magazine's* fiction editor, and an MFA candidate in the University of British Columbia's Creative Writing program. Her poetry has recently appeared or is forthcoming in *Grain, SAD Mag, Cha,* and *Room.* Her play, *Medium*, was staged at the 2017 Brave New Play Rites Festival. Originally from the Philippines, she lives and works in Vancouver.

Jasmine Foong: Digital Media Coordinator
Jasmine Foong is a Malaysian born with a background in journalism and political science. She is currently pursuing her undergraduate degree at UBC, but has formerly worked at Malaysiakini and the Charlatan, with published works in the Ubyssey and Suitcase Magazine. Interested in all things art, Jasmine is an avid reader and documentary-watcher, otherwise much of her time is spent taking photos on her little 35mm camera.

Leila Lee: Non-Fiction Editor
Leila Lee holds a BA (honours) and MA in Canadian and American history. Her research interest lies in exploring "race," racism, and immigration history in North America, with a special focus on Asian communities. She's particularly interested in understanding these issues through a legal and psychoanalytic lens.

William Tham Wai Liang: Creative Non-Fiction Editor
William Tham is an enthusiastic fiction writer whose published works revolve around Malaysia, where he grew up. In collaboration with the independent publisher Fixi Novo, William is hoping to branch out into other topics of interests, particularly with respect to Vancouver and Canada in general. His first novel, *Kings of Petaling Street*, was published by Fixi London.

Yilin Wang: Poetry Editor
Yilin Wang's fiction and poetry have appeared in *Ricepaper Magazine, LooseLeaf Magazine, Cerebration Journal*, and *Abyss & Apex* as well as the anthology *Best of Abyss & Apex Vol. 2*. She has also written about culture

and travel for *Business Insider, Matador Network, The Tyee,* and *Asian Traveller Magazine*. An MFA student in Creative Writing at UBC, she is at work on a high fantasy novel inspired by Chinese folklore. Yilin serves on the Editorial Board at *Room Magazine*. You can find her online at www.yilinwang.com and on Twitter @yilinwriter

Katrina Vera Wong : Managing Editor
Katrina Vera Wong contributes to *Nakid Magazine* and holds editorial positions with *Ricepaper, Discorder, Science Borealis,* and *SAD Mag.* While also volunteering as a marine educator at the Vancouver Aquarium and learning the art of ikebana, she is self-publishing a series of zines that will, in some abstract way, combine art, science and literature. Details and portfolio at www.furiebeckite.com

Gavin Hee: Community Workshop Manager
As *Ricepaper's* Outreach Director, Gavin Hee aims to connect people around the world interested in relatable, meaningful content by Asians. He was born and raised in North Vancouver and spent his formative twenties in Seoul where his concept of multiculturalism transformed. He is particularly fond of pan-Asian themed stories of inter-cultural exchange and he is the founder of weshareinterests. com, a site he thinks you might enjoy since you are reading this. He encourages marginalized voices to build their own world so they are not stuck in someone else's.

Charlotte Nip: Books Editor
Charlotte Nip, born and raised Vancouverite, is an aspiring writer and *Ricepaper Magazine's* current books editor. While pursuing her BA in English Literature at UBC, she devotes her time to new media publications. Some of her experiences include: being published on

ThoughtCatalog and Germ Magazine, working as a managing editor for Spoon University UBC, and currently interning at UBC Press. Follow her daily adventures on Instagram: @charlottenip13

Shuyue He: Editorial Correspondent (Montréal)
Originally from Shanghai, Shuyue He is an inspiring journalist, translator, and political activist. She currently resides in Montréal where she is pursuing a BA Honors degree in Philosophy and History. Her research interests focus on comparative studies of Chinese and Western Philosophy, policy reform in higher education institutes, and historical underpinnings of today's China. At *Ricepaper*, she is in charge of a project focusing on the impact of overseas education on forming a new Chinese identity. After graduation, she intends to go to the U.S or France for graduate school in Public Policy and Chinese studies, where she will gain further experience in relevant fields. She speaks English, Chinese Mandarin, and French.

Priscilla Yu: Art Editor
Priscilla Yu is *Ricepaper Magazine's* art editor. She is a Vancouver- based artist and her projects range from visual arts and illustration to art direction, graphic design, and product design. Her work has been featured on *BOOOOOOOM, Upperplayground, Uppercase Magazine,* and she has exhibited with TEDx Vancouver, FAAIM (Chicago), CO-LAB Gallery (Los Angeles), Robert Lynds Gallery, and Ayden Gallery. You can find her work on www.priscillayu.ca

David Ly: Digital Content Coordinator
David Ly is the Content Coordinator at *Ricepaper,* curating its Instagram, Twitter, and Facebook feeds, driving visitors to the website. He is a Vancouver-based writer, poet, and Master of Publishing graduate from

Simon Fraser University. His journalism has appeared on *Daily Xtra, NUVO,* and *VICE,* and his poetry on *Ricepaper, Westender, The Puritan,* and in the E*rotic Haiku Of Skin On Skinanthology* (Black Moss Press, 2017). His chapbook is titled *A Perfect Jawline* (Anstruther Press, 2018). He is the Marketing Assistant at UBC Press. Find David on Twitter @dlylyly or Instagram @divad.ly

Nick Stember: Translation Editor

Nick Stember is a translator and historian of Chinese comics and science fiction. In 2015 he completed a MA in the UBC Department of Asian Studies. His work has been featured in *The International Journal of Comic Art, Clarkesworld Magazine, Pathlight,* and *LEAP: The International Art Magazine of Contemporary China.* He is currently working closely with: The Jia Pingwa Institute, in Xi'an, to bring more of Jia's work into English; Storycom and The Shimmer Program, to promote Chinese speculative fiction; The Huang Yao Foundation, as a research consultant; and the Books from Taiwan Manhua Project.

Keyan Zhang: Design Editor (Calgary)

Keyan Zhang is currently a graduate student in the Master of Publishing program at Simon Fraser University. She has written and designed for multiple Chinese media companies as a freelancer. As a member of the Calligraphy Association, her calligraphy work has been included in several art publications. She has been worked at Tradewind Books, a Vancouver children's book publishing house, and Indian Summer Arts Society for the summer festival 2017.

Grace Galang: Outreach Coordinator

Grace Galang is a soon-to-be graduate at SFU as an English Major along with a Creative Writing Certificate, and an Asia-Canada Studies

Extended Minor. While she was born in the Philippines, she spent most of her life growing up in Vancouver where during her high school years she developed a growing interest in East Asian culture. Her career aspiration is to become a narrative designer for video games, and currently she is helping to script the story for an indie JRPG in development called Harmonia.

Kathy Nguyen: Research Editor

Kathy Nguyen is a writer with a love for speculative fiction. As an undergraduate student at the University of British Columbia, pursuing a BSc. in Behavioural Neuroscience and a double major in English Literature, she has conducted research in the UBC Child Study Labs concerning the effects of enculturation on adolescent moral development and has developed a keen interest in postcolonial literature. She is immensely grateful to work with the amazing team at *Ricepaper Magazine* and is excited to learn more about the Asian Canadian literary scene. Currently, she writes for the UBC Blog Squad. Kathy is primarily responsible for supporting the Jim Wong-Chu Emerging Writers Award initiative.

JF Garrard: Deputy Editor (Toronto)

JF Garrard is the President of Dark Helix Press, an Indie publisher of Fantasy, Science Fiction, and Raw Non-Fiction. Her background is in Nuclear Medicine and she has a MBA in Marketing and Strategy. She is an editor and writer of speculative fiction (*The Undead Sorceress, Trump Utopia or Dystopia Anthology, Ricepaper Issue 19.3*), non-fiction (*The Literary Elephant*), as well as children's books (*Feeding The Kraken!, 3x Bilingual Series*). She has been a speaker at various conferences on the topics of publishing, marketing, crowd funding, geek topics (science fiction, anime) and healthcare.

More at www.darkhelixpress.com

Winston Le: Literary Events Coordinator (Vancouver)
Winston Le is a Vietnamese-Canadian poet who hails from Langley, BC. He recently completed the Creative Writing Program at Kwantlen Polytechnic University, where he was also the former President of the Kwantlen Creative Writing Guild. His poetry has been featured in literary journals, such as *Misfit Lit, Pulp Magazine,* and has a poem forthcoming in *Ricepaper Magazine.* His most current writing project is a poetry series that both invokes and reinterprets the sociological imagination of Vietnamese wandering souls into spectral tensions within a modern bilingual persona. When not writing, he coordinates literary events and helps engage the writing community as an Outreach Intern for both *Pulp Literature* and *Ricepaper Magazine.*

We also wish to thank our former copyeditor **Lilly Lin** and our former marketing strategist **Yiming Ma** for their hard work.

www.ingramcontent.com/pod-product-compliance
Lightning Source LLC
Chambersburg PA
CBHW061237170626
46809CB00007B/2717

* 9 7 8 1 9 8 8 4 1 6 2 4 3 *